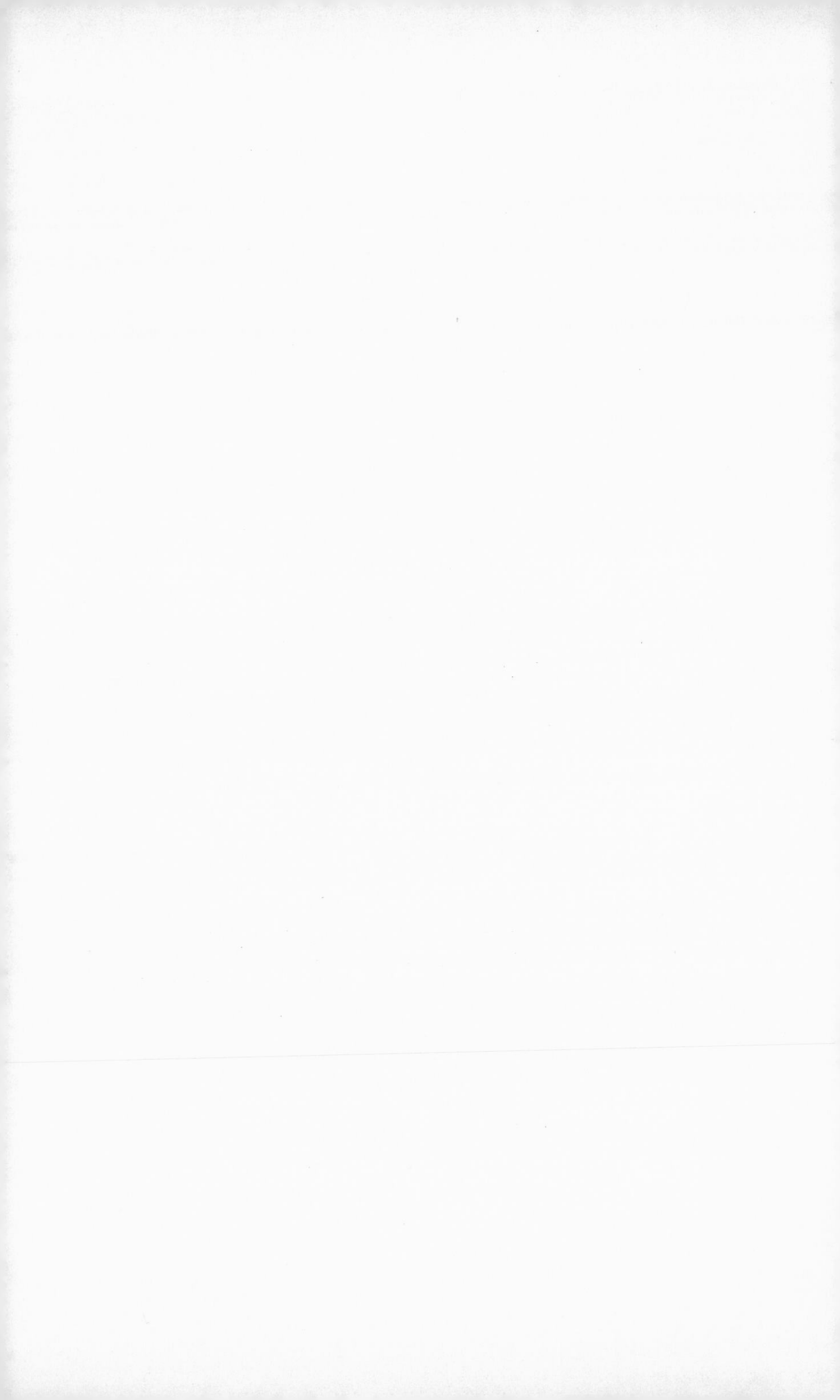

The Secret Road

The Secret Road

ROBERT NORDAN

HOLIDAY HOUSE / New York

For

Joseph Blair

First Edition

Printed in the United States of America

www.holidayhouse.com

Library of Congress Cataloging-in-Publication Data
Nordan, Robert.
The secret road / Robert Nordan.—1st ed.
p. cm.
Summary: Laura leaves her strict parents' Georgia plantation
to spend the summer with her Quaker aunt and uncle,
discovers their home is a stop on the Underground Railroad,
and hatches a dangerous plan to accompany a pregnant slave
to her husband and freedom.
ISBN 0-8234-1543-0 (hardcover)
1. Underground railroad—Juvenile fiction. [1. Underground railroad—Fiction. 2. Fugitive slaves—Fiction. 3. Slavery—Fiction. 4. Quakers—Fiction.] I. Title.

PZ7.N77535 Sg 2001
[Fic]—dc21
00-047294

Table of Contents

Chapter One

Sounds in the Night

Hot. Not a breath of air stirring anywhere. Her hair lay limp on her neck, and her underclothes clung to her body. "Why must I wear them?" she had once asked her mother. But her mother, getting that look on her face, all tense, head drawn back so that her chin almost touched her chest, said, "Why, Laura Milford, what are you saying? No nice girl would ever let a thought like that cross her mind." So every night of summer she went to bed in her stiff cotton underwear, sweltering and praying for a breeze.

Here at her aunt Charity and uncle Jesse's house it was different. She could dash across the fields with the dog barking at her heels, explore the woods, follow Aunt Charity around as she fed the chickens, with no warnings about soiling her clothes or reminders of proper behavior. If she were at home, she would have been sitting demurely in the parlor of some neighboring plantation, with gloves on her hands, sipping tea while her mother and the other ladies gossiped in whispers behind curved fingers. Still, she did not remove her underclothes, afraid that, somehow, her mother would know when she returned home.

She could stand the heat no longer. Flinging aside the covers, she got out of bed and walked across the room to the window. No cooler there, but she could breathe a little easier. The moon lit the yard below, the sandy lot raked smooth by Aunt Charity's twig broom. Insects screeched in the bushes. Beyond loomed the barn, and beside it the chicken coop and the meat house, shadowed now except for the silvery tin roofs that shone through the branches of the giant oak tree where friends hitched their horses when they came to visit.

So much had happened. Just yesterday, she and her brother, Henry, had driven down the narrow road that ended beneath the oak tree. Even before Laura could step down from the chaise and Henry could tie up the horse, Aunt Charity was there, slightly out of breath, her dark clothes rumpled so that she looked like a little puffed-up bird. Uncle Jesse followed along behind her with his slow lanky stride, smiling through his beard.

"Why, child, thou are a sight for sore eyes," Aunt Charity had said, hugging her, and Uncle Jesse gave her a prickly peck on the cheek. Henry, tall now, too grown up to let himself be hugged, shook their hands and said that he would have to be off soon to get back home before dark. But Aunt Charity said she wouldn't hear of it, he'd have to eat some dinner before she'd let him get near that horse again; and he had been persuaded to stay without much trouble, no doubt remembering Aunt Charity's freshly baked cakes and pies.

That morning, her mama had been up at dawn, bustling about. She must have asked a hundred times, "Laura, have you forgotten anything?" and worried Nellie almost to death with questions about the preserves and pecans and salt ham she had packed in a basket to sit on the chaise next to Laura's trunks.

"Yes, ma'am, I tol' you it's all there done up just fine," Nellie had said, but five minutes later her mama would be back, worrying again.

As with most everything these days, she and her mother had argued over Laura's clothes. Weeks before the trip, her mama had pored over Godey's *Lady's Book*, going on about pleats and ruffles and ribbons, while Laura sat bored, wishing she could go outside. And later, at the store in town, she had had to stand by while her mother looked at yard goods and discussed patterns with the storekeeper's wife, finally making her choices to carry home for the dressmaker to cut and sew. "Mama," Laura had said, "it's only Aunt Charity and Uncle Jesse I'm going to see. There won't be any dancing parties with dressed-up folks. It's against their religion. And you know the kind of clothes they wear. Plain, even for church. Those dresses will probably stay in the trunk the whole time I'm there."

"You never know," her mother had said, her neck stiffening. She might have been a board. "They just might have company, some of the neighbors. You're growing up now, Laura. You've got to begin acting like a young lady."

So Laura had spent what seemed like long hours standing on a footstool while the dressmaker turned up hems and her mother stood off to the side, smiling, almost pleased.

Funny how two people could be kin and grow up together but be so unalike: her mama and Aunt Charity, sisters, though you'd never know it by looking. Her mama was tall, slim, wore her hair pulled back in a tight bun on her neck. She gave brief little kisses and no hugs at all, and sometimes Laura thought her mama loved the new set of parlor furniture and the carpet that covered the floor more than she loved her or Henry or even their papa.

But her aunt Charity was different. Short, just an inch or two taller than Laura (who was still growing), she was soft and warm, exuding a scent of dried apples and spice and wood smoke from the hearth. She bubbled with laughter, but the sight of a dead chick in the hen yard could make her eyes watery. Her arms were made for holding small things, a calf, a lamb; but she and Uncle Jesse had no children. *Such a shame,* Laura thought when they hugged and she felt Aunt Charity's quick heartbeat against her chest.

Finally they were ready to leave. Papa had already lifted Laura up beside Henry on the chaise when her mother came running out of the house with a lace collar in her hand, and said in a worried voice, "Laura, you forgot this. I can't take anything for granted around here," and unbuckled one of the trunks and put it inside. Henry rolled his eyes. "Now you be careful, honey," she said to his turned-away face. "Don't stop to talk to strangers." Her father slapped the rump of the horse, Henry flicked the reins, and they rolled away. Nellie waved good-bye from the porch.

The sun was still low in the heavens, hidden by the far trees, but the sky was turning a pure gold that promised searing heat by midmorning. On both sides of the road cotton fields spread out. Field hands were just beginning to come to work, dark figures bent and slow-moving, only a face or two turning to watch them pass. At the edge of the field beneath the shade of a tree, a girl much younger than Laura sat watching two small children playing in the dirt; she cradled another, just a baby, in her arms. Their mothers would come to feed them when they had a dinner break from work.

"You are never to go to the slave quarters," her father had told her years ago. "They're no place for a girl."

"Why not, Papa?" she'd said in a piping tone, used to having her way with him.

"Because I said so," he answered in an iron voice, and she knew not to push him further. It was the worst possible thing to tell her, of course. She had to see for herself. So one hot summer afternoon, while her mother napped and even the flies were still, she slipped out of the house and ran across the yard to the winding road that led past the barns and hog pens to the cabins where the slaves lived. No one was about, and she crept up to the window of the nearest cabin. At first she saw only blackness, but then in the light coming through the open doorway, she could make out the mud-chinked walls, the dirt floor, the broken table and chair that sat there. A few pieces of clothing hung on wall pegs, and there was a glimmer of cooking pots in the fire-place. Nothing at all unusual, and, disappointed, she wondered about her father's prohibitions. What was he afraid she would see there? She could not ask, of course, and afterward she rarely noticed those cabins that sat hidden behind a stand of trees at the edge of the fields.

"Morning, Master Henry. Miss." Mr. Hawes, the overseer, rode up to them, and Henry reined in the horses. Mr. Hawes tipped his hat. A big man, he wore heavy leather boots summer and winter and a coat that was worn and stained in places. He smelled like the stables. Mr. Hawes was the one who roused the field hands in the morning with the blast of a horn, the one who decided when a woman could go back to the fields after she birthed a child. Though Laura had never seen it in his hand, a whip lay across the saddle in front of him. She did not want to think of its use.

"Morning, Mr. Hawes." Henry, silent until then, was angry, Laura knew, because he had to drive her all the way to Aunt Charity and Uncle Jesse's house. Henry sometimes rode out with Mr. Hawes—their papa's orders, though Henry didn't seem to mind—sitting straight in the saddle, listening intently to whatever Mr. Hawes might be telling him.

Henry had changed so much in the past year. Gone were the days when he would come running to find her and then half drag her along the edge of the woods, whispering, "Quiet, quiet, don't frighten them, it's a nest of cardinals. Look." No longer did he bring her a silvery cocoon woven on a dry branch or an abandoned wasps' nest with papery sides. Now the only time he seemed happy was when he went with other boys in the cool of the morning to fish and hunt, bringing home a string of dead birds and squirrels for Nellie to cook.

"Going to be a hot one." Mr. Hawes pulled out a handkerchief and wiped his brow. "The niggers are already sweating." He laughed, then turned to Laura. "Where are you off to, miss? Far?"

She didn't answer him at first, her eyes on the whip in front of him. "To my aunt and uncle's," she said. "I go to visit them every summer. Henry used to go along, too."

Henry shrugged, and Mr. Hawes laughed and said, "He's got work to do here, I guess. Cotton's coming right along. We needed another man around the place."

Laura could have hit him. Henry was already swollen up, proud as a peacock most of the time, and Mr. Hawes's words would only make him worse. She was ignored, of course, a *girl.* Who could expect anything from her unless it was a task in the kitchen or a tune on the piano in the parlor?

They rode in silence after that. When the sun was fully up, burning, the sky thinned out to a pale blue. A few crows circled near the treetops, dark as midnight, and a flutter of sparrows rose up from the woods as they passed. Drops of sweat tickled Laura's neck and darkened her collar. Finally she said to Henry, "Can't we stop for a while? I'm burning up. And we've got all that food Nellie packed for us."

He didn't answer, just gave a grunt, but the next time they passed a clearing in the woods, he slowed the horse and turned the chaise from the road. Laura jumped down, relieved, already cooler beneath the trees, with soft pine needles under her feet and the sound of a stream nearby. She took down the basket of food, spread a cloth on the ground, and uncovered the plate of chicken Nellie had fried that morning before daylight.

They ate without speaking, for a brief time content. Henry lay back, his eyes closed and legs stretched out, and in a moment he was gently snoring. Laura watched the rise and fall of his chest, saw one leg twitch, and smiled, remembering how proud he had been the day he got his first pair of long trousers and strutted around for her to admire. She had loved him so back then. And now he was almost a grown man, or thought so, anyway, with a small patch of reddish hair thinner than a bird's breast on his upper lip and a horse and a gun of his own, riding out with Mr. Hawes. Would he, too, someday carry a whip?

He roused then, stretched, brushed back his hair, and said, "I guess we'd better be on our way." He picked up the basket and took it back to the chaise.

The rest of the trip had been uneventful. They passed no one else on the road, and the few houses they saw looked almost deserted, closed up against the heat of the afternoon. Once a child waved, and from beneath a porch a couple of dogs came snapping at the wheels of the chaise until they fell back, eyes filled with dust, panting.

"There!" Laura said suddenly. "That stand of trees." She pointed down the road that rose gently and ended at a point above Uncle Jesse's farm.

And then there it was, spread out before them as neat as a sampler, the weathered brown house, the kitchen garden, the bright patch of flowers Aunt Charity grew for pure pleasure, the plowed fields, and the woods beyond. Henry jerked the reins and speeded up, as eager as she to arrive. They bounced down the hill, dust rising in a cloud behind them, to stop under the giant oak tree near the barn, with Aunt Charity already calling, "Welcome, welcome!" as she came rushing from the house to greet them.

Still no cooler. The thin white curtains Aunt Charity had made to brighten the little upstairs room did not move, and Laura's underclothes lay damp upon her back. The night was darker. The moon had slipped off somewhere, and the raked white sand beneath the window was shadowed with blue. Soon dawn would come streaking across the sky, and birds would begin to sing. Laura sighed, turning to look at the narrow rumpled bed. She should try to sleep again. Work on the farm began early, and though Aunt Charity never called up the stairs to wake her in the morning, Laura felt she could not lie asleep while her aunt hurried about the stifling kitchen making breakfast. She gave one last look out the window before stepping toward the bed.

Then she heard the sound.

High, mournful, like a funeral wail, it came from somewhere far off in the darkness, a sound that Laura had heard before back home when she roused in the night. Once, next morning, she had asked, "What was that noise last night, Papa?" but his eyes closed over as if curtains had been drawn behind them, and he had answered, "Nothing for you to worry about, Laura, nothing a-tall," and she knew it would be useless to ask him more.

There it was again, farther off, held like the last note of a hymn in church on a Sunday morning. Bending, she looked out the window, but all was in darkness. Nothing moved. She stood there a moment longer and then quite suddenly felt a chill on the back of her neck, as if a breeze had blown by, though the curtains still lay limp on the windowsill and the only movement in the trees was the first stirring of birds.

Still cool, Laura turned back to her bed, threw aside the covers, and tried to sleep.

Chapter Two

A Light in the Darkness

"Well, Laura, did thou have a good sleep last night?" Uncle Jesse sounded somber, but a smile lurked beneath the frizzled beard that covered most of his face.

"Yes, sir," Laura said, head down, standing at the foot of the stairs in the kitchen, embarrassed. Despite her restlessness, she had finally fallen asleep last night and did not wake until it was far too light and she could hear Aunt Charity bustling around down below getting breakfast. Splashing tepid water on her face from the bowl on the washstand, she had dressed quickly and gone downstairs, where Uncle Jesse sat drinking tea at the kitchen table and Aunt Charity finished up her cleaning.

"Ah, leave the child be," Aunt Charity said, though it was obvious that Uncle Jesse was only teasing. "Seat thyself and eat, Laura. Breakfast is warming by the fire. And thou can scoot," she said to Uncle Jesse. "No need to sit here all day when there's work to do." He laughed, then stood up, tipped his hat to them, and went out the door.

"That man," Aunt Charity said, and shook her head.

While Laura sat at the table, Aunt Charity bent toward the fire that had already turned the kitchen hot to take up a tin bowl of mush and milk and a piece of bacon. She placed them in front of Laura. Laura, still embarrassed, began to eat, knowing, even though there was no clock in the house, that it was quite late.

Too, she was not yet used to Uncle Jesse and Aunt Charity's manner of speaking. "Why do they talk in such a way?" her mama had asked her papa years ago when her aunt and uncle had made one of their rare visits to the plantation. "Theeing and thouing each other, it just doesn't seem natural to me."

"Following the Bible," he had answered, "or at least they think they are. You know the Quakers, don't go along half with what anybody else does. If you didn't want to hear that kind of talk, you should have kept your sister from getting mixed up with them."

Her mother had looked as mad as a setting hen. It was an old family story how she and Aunt Charity, young girls, had traveled from their home on a boat down the river to another farm for a big barbecue, with everybody for miles around invited. Uncle Jesse had been there, too, a stranger, a friend of one of the sons, standing on the sidelines, maybe a little self-conscious in his countrified clothes and beard. "Charity made a beeline for him soon as she set eyes on him, I don't know why," her mother had said. "She was such a pretty thing back then, could have had anybody she wanted. Why she picked Jesse Buchanan I'll never know."

But Laura thought she knew why. Uncle Jesse was a quiet man who handled the animals on his farm gently, one who never raised his voice or swore, and somehow Aunt Charity must have recognized those qualities in him when she stepped off the boat at the barbecue. They had a short courtship, no need to wait with harvest coming on, and Nellie had spent every daylight hour that could be spared from household tasks sewing on her trousseau. Charity's mama, Laura's grandmother, had gathered up linens and cooking pots for her to take to her new home. "Mama," Charity had said, "he's got his own farm, left by his mama and daddy when they died," but it didn't comfort her mother, and she worried and fretted right up to the wedding day.

Usually after a day or so Laura became accustomed to Aunt Charity and Uncle Jesse's speech. She liked going to the meetinghouse with them on Sunday mornings, where they greeted others in the same friendly way, content to sit mostly in silence until the Spirit urged someone to speak. A kind of peace would spread over them all, like a warm blanket on a winter's night, even though babies would whine from time to time and dogs wandered in and out the open door.

"Let me do it," Laura said as Aunt Charity whisked her bowl off the table and began to wash it in a pan of hot water poured from the kettle over the fire.

"Rest," Aunt Charity said to her, smiling. "Thou must be tired still from the ride." She paused a moment, then said, "Did thou sleep last night? It was hot enough to smother, no breeze a-tall."

Laura would never have told Aunt Charity about her restlessness, the sounds she had heard in the night. "I was fine," she said. "Don't worry about me."

Aunt Charity finished the washing up and dried her hands. "Thou can help me," she said, reaching for a basket that sat on the windowsill. "Thy favorite chore, or was when thou was here before."

"The eggs?" Laura stood up, hand out, ready to take the basket.

Aunt Charity laughed. "I see thou remembers. And not afraid, even though thou was attacked by a hen?"

Laura laughed, too. Years ago, when she was just a little girl, Aunt Charity had first taken her out to the henhouse to gather eggs. Stretching high on her tiptoes to reach the row of nests, she had taken the eggs from beneath the setting hens and then carefully placed them in Aunt Charity's basket, her hands folded as if in prayer. They all squawked, the hens, when she disturbed them, but then suddenly one spread its wings, flew up, and landed, cackling, on Laura's head. With a scream she dropped the egg, while Aunt Charity shooed away the chicken. The hen, still grumbling, watched with beady eyes as Aunt Charity wiped away Laura's tears and led her back to the house.

"I won't be long," Laura said. She took the basket and went outside, and Aunt Charity returned to her work.

It was late, the sun already high up in the sky, still no breeze. The white sand of the yard reflected the light, turning bits of mica into diamonds. With her hand held up to shield her eyes, Laura stood on the edge of the porch, scanning the fields, but she saw no one, not even Uncle Jesse or the one old man, Ebenezer, who helped him on the farm. There were no slaves. "They've given them their freedom." She remembered her mama's scandalized voice years ago when she came into the room where Papa sat reading, a letter from Aunt Charity fluttering in her hands. "They'd better be careful," her papa had replied. "Some folks don't like other folks treating their slaves too good."

Laura walked down the steps and out into the yard. The heat struck her bare head and at almost the same instant a reddish blur nearly knocked her down—Ninevah, Uncle Jesse's old dog, rushing from his usual spot in the shade beneath the porch to greet her. Except for Uncle Jesse, Ninevah had little to do with anyone else, even Aunt Charity, who fed him at the kitchen door, but Laura was different. From the time she was a toddler, Ninevah had taken her for his own whenever they visited, tugging at her sashes if she strayed too far, growling if a stranger came too near. She bent and hugged him now, and he responded with happy licks at her face.

They walked together across the yard down to where the thick branches of the oak tree promised shade. Last year's acorns crackled beneath their feet. The chicken house was off to the right, next to the lot where Aunt Charity's cows stood silently chewing and flicking flies with their tails, but Laura couldn't keep away from the barn. Aunt Charity wouldn't mind if she tarried a few minutes before returning with the eggs. She walked to the heavy door, lifted the bar that held it closed, and let the door swing open. The dry scent of hay made her sneeze, and she stood a moment before climbing inside, waiting for her eyes to adjust to the dark interior.

She was looking for kittens. Nearly always, when she came for a visit, she would find a litter there hidden beneath straw in a shadowy corner, the mother stretched out, mewing tiredly while the tiny kittens, eyes still glued together, scrambled across her body in search of a nipple. Ninevah would sit beside her, watching as carefully as she, nudging a kitten back with his big black nose if it fell away. The mother cat was unafraid.

But this time Ninevah pulled away from her, went running through the aisle between bales of hay to the back of the barn where she could not see. "Now come back here, mister," she called to him. "There may be snakes." But he scratched on the wall and whined, and finally Laura, giving up the search for kittens, began to move toward him. She could see better now, see the outlines of the hay bales, straps of old harness hung on nails high up on the walls. And then the smell hit her, the sharpness of salt and cured meat, and she knew where she stood. The meat house was attached to the barn behind the wall next to her. Ninevah stopped scratching, listening. Laura didn't move, suddenly afraid for no reason she could think of.

Then she heard the voice, low, full, like the rumbling of far-off thunder. Uncle Jesse, surely. Who else could it be? She turned, ready to go outside and greet him, but then she heard another voice, lighter this time, almost a whisper. Ninevah gave a low growl. "You shush," she told him, relieved. "It's just Uncle Jesse and Ebenezer working next door. Come on, we'll go see."

She turned and Ninevah followed her outside. The light was dazzling after the darkness of the barn, and she waited a moment by the doorway until she could see again. Gradually the world came back together—the house off in the distance, the two bright pink crape myrtles in the yard, the spreading oak and the hen-house, Ninevah at her feet. She started around the side of the barn toward the meat house door.

She'd never liked it there. It wasn't just the scent of salt that bristled in her nose and made her sneeze, but the sight of the carcasses hung up in the rafters was discomforting—fat hams and slabs of bacon wrapped in cheesecloth. Once, years ago, when she had visited during hog-killing time, she had realized in one horrifying moment that the pigs she had fed just the day before were to be slaughtered, and she ran to the empty parlor and buried her head beneath a cushion on Aunt Charity's hard horsehair sofa, not wanting anyone to see her tears. Even then, she was able to hear the gunshots when they came. For a week afterward she refused to eat any meat, but with the smell of Aunt Charity's good cooking, the memory faded, and soon she was sopping up the red gravy from a thick piece of fried ham as hungrily as before. Still, she did not like the smell of the meat house, and she turned her head from the shadowy forms hanging there whenever she passed the opened door.

"Well, my goodness, Laura. Where did thou come from?" Uncle Jesse seemed surprised to see her, his eyes narrowed behind his spectacles. He quickly closed the meat house door behind him, then turned and drew the heavy bar across. Ninevah went over and sniffed at his feet. Uncle Jesse pushed him away. "What has thou been doing?" he questioned her again.

"We were in the barn, looking for kittens," she said. "Are there any this year?"

Uncle Jesse laughed and shook his head, the surprised look gone. "Not that I know of." He stopped beside her, his clothes smelling slightly rancid from the meat, then headed back toward the house. "Come," he said. "Thy aunt should have dinner ready soon. I need to wash or thou will not be able to stand me at the table."

"What about Ebenezer?" Laura said without thinking. Surely Uncle Jesse wouldn't have slid the bar across the meat house door if Ebenezer was still inside.

Uncle Jesse waited a moment before he replied. "What *about* Ebenezer?"

"I thought I—" Laura stopped before all the words were out. *I thought I heard you talking to him in the meat house,* she was going to say, but the look on Uncle Jesse's face, his eyes smooth as the surface of water, told her not to.

"Ebenezer is clearing off some brush over in the

west field," Uncle Jesse continued as if she had not spoken. "He said to give thee his greetings."

They were silent as they walked back to the house, the sun hot on their necks, their feet making little puffs of dust in the sand. Ninevah ran ahead, and when they arrived at the porch, he had already lapped up the bowl of water Aunt Charity had left there for him. Uncle Jesse pulled off his outer shirt and began to wash up. It wasn't until she went inside the kitchen and looked down at the empty basket in her hand that Laura realized she had forgotten to gather the eggs.

Uncle Jesse and Aunt Charity took a nap every afternoon after dinner. With the bedcovers carefully folded back, they lay upon the sheets, waking an hour later, refreshed, ready to work again till nearly dark.

Laura tried. She went to her room upstairs, but it was more stifling than it had been the night before. For a while she lay in the hammock stretched between two China trees in the front yard, but the birds were noisy in the top branches and still there was no breeze. Finally she sat down on the top step of the porch, not concerned about her skirt, and stared at the layers of heat that wavered above the fields.

"Poor boy," she said to Ninevah as he slowly emerged from beneath the steps, panting. She poured him some more water from the bucket, and he came up on the porch and drank a few mouthfuls, then sat down beside her. "Maybe I should give you a good dunking," she said, and laughed.

Then she remembered the creek in the woods down behind the barn. It bubbled over smooth stones no matter how dry it was. She and Henry had caught minnows in its pools while Ninevah ran and splashed. She could let him play there again. And with no one else to see (though she could hear her mother's voice telling her it wasn't at all ladylike), she could remove her shoes and stockings and wade into the stream. Ninevah stood up, stretched, then started down the steps as if he knew. Laura followed him.

Again they walked through the heat of the yard to the barn, then past it, past the meat house, down a rocky hillside where nothing grew except scrub brush, and to the woods. A kind of path led in, and as soon as they bent beneath the branches, they could feel a slight cooling of the air.

Ninevah urged her on, his plumed tail wagging along the rocky way, and suddenly they came upon the stream. With a bark, the dog plunged in, scattering drops in the sunlight, and Laura, her mother's warning voice only a faint echo in her head, sat on the bank, pulled off her shoes and stockings, and, with her skirts held high, walked into the water. Its coolness almost took her breath away.

She lost all track of time. The leaves filtered the light and the overhanging growth darkened the stream, and after she climbed out of the water and sat on the bank with her legs stretched out in a patch of sun to dry, she must have dozed. Returning birds startled her awake. Quickly she sat up, put on her stockings and shoes, and, calling to Ninevah, turned back along the faint path.

But he did not follow her. She heard no excited yelp, no swish of his tail against dry leaves. "Where is that dog?" she said aloud and called to him again. He was perfectly capable of finding his way home, but suddenly there in the darkening wood she wanted him by her side. She turned back to the stream, calling, "Ninevah. Ninevah?" but still got no response.

She walked a little ways upstream. A fall of rocks blocked her view and made her going rougher, but when she rounded the outermost edge, she still did not find the dog. "Ninevah?" she called once more, and recognized the worry in her voice. Then she heard his bark, quite near in fact. Rushing, her skirts forgotten, she hurried along the water's edge, deeper there, and found him behind a pile of stones. "Bad dog!" she said, but he just stood looking at her, eyes gleaming, and did not move.

"Come," she said, turning back along the way she had come, but she did not hear a splash behind her or a rolling of pebbles down the hill, and she looked around again. He had disappeared. "Ninevah!" she said, angry this time, ready to go back to the house, suddenly tired there in the woods. He poked his head through an opening in the bank, dead leaves and the roots of young trees framing his face, then jerked back. *Come look,* he seemed to say, and, curious now, she lifted her skirts and stepped across the stream on a path of stones.

She held on to branches to pull herself up the hill. Her skirts might tear, but she had to see what Ninevah wanted to show her. She pushed through the opening, caught her hair on a briar, and jerked away, almost crying out from the pain. Clods of dirt slid down her collar. But finally, with Ninevah licking her face, she was there, tumbled onto the rocky floor of a cave.

The cave was quite large. If she watched her head, she could stand up in it. "Well, Mr. Ninevah," she said, teasing, "you've certainly made a discovery," and he jumped about as if he recognized her praise.

She got up. She couldn't go back now. She had to explore the cave or it would linger in her mind all day and night like an itch she couldn't get to. With Ninevah walking ahead of her, she moved carefully across the rocks to the far side of the cave and discovered, now that her eyes had adjusted, that it was not in complete darkness. Narrow strips of light came from above where an animal's paw had scattered stones away or a root had pushed down deep inside. Careful not to bump her head, she began to walk farther, finding the going quite easy now, the floor smooth.

The light dimmed as she continued on, but still she was able to find her way by the sudden flickers that came from above. Perhaps she should have been afraid, but it was excitement that made her heart beat faster, and she could not turn back. Anyway, Ninevah was with her—surely he would not lead her into danger.

Then he stopped, a low growl in his throat. She almost stumbled over him. "What is it?" she whispered, peering ahead into total darkness. He brushed up against her leg and she reached down to pat his head. "Let's go, boy," she said, her voice still soft. Ninevah whined but moved away from her, and she slowly walked ahead, with only the glow of the light behind her to guide the way.

She felt a turning of the cave and for a moment was lost in utter blackness, then she saw the light ahead, a bright square of wavering gold. At first she thought it must be an opening to the daylight above, but as she moved closer, she saw that it was a window, a small square in a heavy door, its planks warped by moisture.

Then she smelled the scent, sharp enough to burn her nose, the salt smell of preserved meat, and she suddenly knew where she stood. She was beneath Uncle Jesse's meat house. She had made her way through a cave behind the rocky hillside near the barn, where no one ever plowed and only rabbits scampered. Perhaps that was how Ninevah had discovered the cave and its opening. He had chased a rabbit into a hole, followed it, and tumbled onto the hard-packed floor of the cave. But others must have known of its existence. The way was well-trodden; the opening, though hidden, easily accessible if you knew which vines to pull aside.

She was aware of her footsteps, tried to muffle them as she hurried toward the bright window. Ninevah's pads made no sound, though he whined slightly as she moved in front of him, eager to see what was ahead. She held her breath, as if the sound of her breathing might suddenly make all this disappear.

At first she thought nothing was there, just a small square room with a dirt floor and a mound of straw in the corner. A table, a chair, a flickering candle flame. Then she saw movement in the straw. A bare foot emerged, arms, fingers brushing back dark hair. And finally a face, golden in the candlelight, a girl no more than a year or two older than Laura herself, her eyes still heavy with sleep. Laura, in her surprise, gasped, "Oh!" and the sound startled the girl. Her eyes widened, she looked around, and then she must have seen Laura's face in the window. Ninevah barked once and began to scrape frantically at the door.

The expression on the girl's face was one of horror. Laura might have been some devil emerging from the darkness. Pulling at the straw as if she could cover herself again and find peace once more in sleep, the girl drew back and said to Laura in a trembling voice, "Please don't hurt me, miss! Take away the dogs. Please don't let them get me!"

Chapter Three

Answers

Laura waited till after supper to ask them. Uncle Jesse, seated at the kitchen table, had just lit a pipe, and Aunt Charity was washing up. Laura brought in one more bucket of water, filled the kettle hanging in the fireplace, and then set the bucket outside the door.

"Lord, I do hope we get some rain soon," Aunt Charity said, brushing back a strand of hair that had escaped the bun at the nape of her neck, her face shiny in the late afternoon light. "Everything is burning up."

"No sign," Uncle Jesse said, blowing smoke into the air. "The almanac said it was going to be a hot summer, and it's usually right."

Laura could stand it no longer, the three of them sitting there talking as if it were any other night with nothing more mysterious in the air than the flock of dark birds that returned at sundown to roost in the oak tree by the barn. "Who is she?" she asked, even though she knew she might incur their wrath. "The girl beneath the meat house. What is she doing there?"

She could have asked the girl, of course, could have said, "Who are you? What are you doing here?" But the sight of her there on a pile of straw beneath the floor of the meat house, weeping and pleading for mercy, had so frightened her that she'd turned from the opening in the door and run back through the cave until she was outside again. Ninevah had stood patiently in the water, his coat darkened by the stream. "Come," she said to him, fearful of stopping, and the two of them hurried through the woods until they came out at the edge of the field.

But Laura could not walk up that rocky hill now that she knew what lay beneath, the dark cave ending in the room under the meat house. If she walked there, she would fear with every step that her foot would plunge through the surface and she herself would be caught, another prisoner with straw to lie on and a candle to give a feeble light. Following the edge of the woods, she came to the orchard and bent beneath the boughs of the apple trees that grew there. Ninevah, hoping, perhaps, that she would pull one of the hard green apples from a branch and toss it for him to catch, plunged through the weeds ahead of her and then stood waiting. "No," she told him, and sank down beneath a tree.

She couldn't go back to face them yet, Aunt Charity and Uncle Jesse. Questions flew about her head like the yellow jackets that darted at the fruit lying upon the ground. *Who is the girl beneath the meat house? What is she doing there? Do Aunt Charity and Uncle Jesse know?* But then she thought, *Of course they do. That was the voice I heard this morning when I was in the barn. Uncle Jesse was talking to the girl there.* Worst of all, he had lied to her, that faraway look in his eyes as he came out of the meat house door and pretended no one was in there. Uncle Jesse, an elder of the church who presided over meetings and who, she would have said before, had never intentionally done one sinful thing in his entire life.

She didn't know how long she stayed there. The sun sank lower in the sky, Ninevah gave up hope of playing and lay down by her side, the yellow jackets flew away. She might have dozed. Finally she heard the back door slam and realized she had to go in. They would be calling her soon. "Come on," she said to Ninevah, getting up and shaking out her wrinkled, dirtied skirt. "Let's go back to the house." He bounced ahead once again, and she followed him from beneath the boughs.

She was able to get up the kitchen stairs without Aunt Charity's noticing her clothes. "We'll eat soon," Aunt Charity said, kneeling at the hearth's edge to take a pan of bread from the fire as Laura hurried by. Once in her room, Laura changed her dress and washed her face in the bowl of water Aunt Charity had replenished on the washstand. Her hair was wild, and she tried, as best she could, to smooth it down.

She went downstairs again, quiet, avoiding their eyes. "We thank Thee for this food," Uncle Jesse prayed when they sat down at the table, and Laura peeked at him through half-closed eyes, wondering how he could sit there and talk to God when he had lied to her about the girl in the meat house. She had no appetite, and pushed her food around on her plate until Aunt Charity finally said, "Are thou sick, Laura? Did thou get overheated today?"

"No, no," she told her, but said no more.

Finally they were finished. With Laura's help, Aunt Charity cleaned up the dishes, and Uncle Jesse went to sit in his chair by the window where his Bible lay, sweet pipe smoke winding around his head. It was then that Laura asked her question.

For a minute there was no sound in the room, as if all three held their breath, waiting. Then a log broke in the fireplace, shooting sparks, and they breathed out again, released. With her face turned toward the window, Aunt Charity said quietly, "Thou knows?" and Uncle Jesse put the big Bible on his knees and rested his hands there.

"I heard you talking to somebody while I was in the barn," she said to Uncle Jesse without meeting his eyes.

"Then I saw you coming from the meat house, and you said nobody was there. I believed you."

Uncle Jesse sighed and placed his pipe on the table by his chair. "Indeed, I did not tell thee the truth," he said. "I am sorry, Laura. God would not have me do so. Thou surprised me. I did not know what else to say at that moment."

Before Laura could answer, Aunt Charity turned from the table where the dishes lay, wiped her hands on her apron, and said, "Poor child. Perhaps we should not have had thee come this year." She reached out and took Laura's hand. "We did not plan to make thee a part of this. We had no word that she would come. But then she found us, and we could not turn her away."

"But who *is* she?" Laura asked again. "Why is she hiding in the cave?"

Uncle Jesse gave a start. "Thou found the cave, too?"

"Ninevah did. We went into the woods to cool off by the creek. He went exploring and I went to find him and he showed me the opening. I saw her. I saw the girl there. Then I ran."

"Thou need not have been afraid," Uncle Jesse said, almost as if he could feel the sudden rapid beating of her heart that came with the memory of the girl lying in candlelight. He laid aside the Bible, stood up the way he sometimes did on Sundays in the meetinghouse, but did not speak. Instead he went to stand by Aunt Charity, first looking through the window out across the fields so that Laura wondered if he, too, might not have some fear. It was Aunt Charity who finally told her, giving her hand a squeeze before she let go.

"She is a slave," Aunt Charity said, "come away from her master. She's been on the road now for days, living on whatever she could find in the woods—berries, roots. Dogs were after her. She barely escaped, but with guidance from others she found her way here."

"Why?" Laura asked, thinking of Nellie back home and the other women who helped her mother in the house. They would not run away. The field hands she had never seen mistreated, though she *had* seen the notices tacked up on the trunks of trees or the courthouse wall when she went to town to shop with her mama. WANTED! RUNAWAY SLAVE, they said, and there would be a face drawn beneath the letters. She'd paid them little attention as she passed by.

Aunt Charity turned to look at Uncle Jesse, her eyes asking him to speak. "Ah, child," he said in a low voice. He smiled gently at her as if she had been just a little girl, but his voice held an echo of sadness. "Thou has been protected. Thy papa is a good man, and perhaps thou has not witnessed slaves being beaten, heard the cries of mothers separated from their children, gone hungry and cold in winter darkness. Thou has not seen the scars of whips, bandaged the bites of dogs. But it happens to others. That is why she is here, the girl you saw. To escape all that, to find her way to freedom."

There was silence in the room. Outside, the sun touched the tops of the trees with fire, and flocks of birds rustled in the branches, cawing. Uncle Jesse and Aunt Charity seemed to be waiting for Laura to speak, but her mind was as confused as the cries of the birds, and she found no words. Was it possible? Were the slaves on her papa's farm treated in such a way and she had never realized? It was true that she had seen no beatings, never heard a mother's cry for her lost child. But she *had* seen Mr. Hawes fingering his whip at the edge of the field, had peered into the miserable cabins where the slaves laid their tired bodies when they returned home at sunset. She had heard the cries of dogs.

Aunt Charity seemed to understand her confusion. "We believe all are the same," she explained. "All share God's inner light, no one better than another. So no one has the right to own a person, to treat them like chattel. That's why the girl is here. She's not the first to come."

"How did she know? How to find you, I mean."

Uncle Jesse's spectacles reflected the setting sun. "There are signs people leave," he said. "Hatchet marks on the side of a tree, stones piled a certain way, lantern lights to signal. There are many of us who do this work, people all over. Some say it's like a railroad, an underground railroad that picks up people and carries them from one station to another on their way to freedom."

He sighed. "We lose many," he said. "There are slave catchers. Slaves betray other slaves for money. The neighbors are suspicious of us since I let our people go. Some folks have even been tarred and feathered and driven away. But we keep on. God will protect us. It is His will."

Again there was silence, though a sense of peace prevailed in the room. The birds outside had quieted, too, and the sky had turned a peach color, gradually fading. There might have even been a breeze. Aunt Charity stirred, hands fluttering beneath her apron. "She will be hungry," she said, nodding toward the meat house. "Will thou bring her in now?" she asked Uncle Jesse.

"Yes," he said. "It will be dark soon and the moon is slow to rise." He moved closer to Laura. "Will thou come? Thou need not be afraid this time. Rosetta will not bite thee."

"Rosetta?"

"Yes, Rosetta. The girl in the meat house. Rosetta is her name."

Chapter Four

The Hidden Room

They waited till the final color left the sky and the first stars appeared. "It'll be ready when thou returns," Aunt Charity said to Uncle Jesse and Laura, fixing a plate of cold hominy and side meat and gravy for the girl. "She was starved half to death when she got here," she told Laura. "What little bit of food she could carry with her when she left was long gone, and she'd had nothing else to eat except berries and the green apples she could snatch from the trees."

"You're going to bring her to the house?" Laura said. Till now, the girl beneath the meat house had been like a story told, a dream recounted, even though she had seen her that one instant before she turned and ran in fear.

The thought of her as a real person, with a name, hungry and ready to eat, gave Laura a fluttery feeling inside, as if, stepping out onto the porch with Uncle Jesse, she was embarking on a strange journey that could somehow change her life.

"It should be safe," Uncle Jesse said, answering her question. "Thou knows now. We don't have to hide her from thy eyes. And the neighbors will be in bed. We'll have no lights. The stars are enough for us to see by. Come."

They walked down the steps. There was a rustle beneath the porch and Ninevah slid out, stretched, and began to pad along beside them. "Thou are a good dog," Uncle Jesse said and patted his head. Ninevah wagged his tail but made no sound. Their own steps were silent, muffled by the sand. When she spoke, Laura did so in a whisper, as if they told ghost stories in the dark. "Uncle Jesse, how did it get there, the room at the end of the cave? Who made it?"

"God," he said, and his voice, too, was quiet. "Thousands of years ago all the land behind the barn was a river. Now it is only a creek, higher during spring rains, but low in summer. Back, though, when there were only wild creatures to see, the heavier waters washed through, washed stones and dirt away. The cave was created, the entrance grown over, and probably no one knew for years. Then, maybe someone came along like thee and Ninevah and discovered it. My father, my grandfather, and probably others before them. My grandfather decided to build the meat house over it for protection. The meat could be hidden there from animals. People could be hidden there if Indians came. Now it has a different purpose."

Suddenly Uncle Jesse stopped speaking and gave a low whistle. It might have been a mockingbird. No answer came that Laura heard, but they walked on, past the entrance to the barn and the chicken coop, to the meat house. Uncle Jesse undid the heavy bar, and the door swung open. It was pitch dark inside, but they lit no light. Moving slowly, like someone blind, Uncle Jesse made his way across the floor while Laura waited outside. She heard a creak and a grunt from Uncle Jesse, then saw a narrow band of light.

Uncle Jesse raised the trapdoor to the hidden room, then reached around and found a ladder and dropped it into the hole. "Hurry, child, come up," he said. "Thou need not be afraid." And he reached forward into the light, the muscles in his forearms taut as roots beneath the ground, and tried to catch the pair of hands fluttering there.

"Yes sir," came a voice. Still standing in the doorway, Laura peered into the blackness but could see nothing, not even a shadow. She heard a scuffling sound, then the door falling heavily back into place. Until that moment she had forgotten that Ninevah sat behind her heels, but he suddenly stood and gave a low growl as he had done before in the cave.

"Quiet!" Uncle Jesse said sternly, and Ninevah moved back once more.

They appeared in the doorway, Uncle Jesse and the girl. Rosetta. She leaned on him as if she had no strength to walk. "Help her," Uncle Jesse told Laura. "I have to bar the door." He guided the girl's hands to Laura's.

Laura almost drew back. *"If you touch them wash right away,"* she remembered her mother's warning. *"They have a scent."* But when she moved closer to Rosetta, all she smelled was dusty weeds, salt, the summer sun—nothing strange—so she put her arms around the girl's shoulders and said, "Come this way." Ninevah moved ahead, quiet, and Uncle Jesse closed the door and followed them down the path to the barn. When they reached the light, the girl straightened up, pulled away, and said in a stronger voice, "Thank you, miss. I'll be just fine now. You don't need to trouble."

Laura let her go, stepped back, and looked at her really for the first time. *Why, she's pretty!* she thought. In the starlight Rosetta's pale skin glowed and her hair fell down her back in ringlets. Her eyes were a strange pale gray, like still water in a shadowy pool. Take off the raggedy clothes, put her in a decent dress, give her shoes and stockings, and she would look hardly different from the girls Mama took Laura to visit on Sunday afternoons back home.

They walked quickly back to the house, Uncle Jesse on one side of the girl, Laura on the other. Ninevah followed. It was lighter now, the moon about to rise, and when they reached the porch the girl walked just a little faster, hurrying up the steps as if she wanted again the cover of darkness.

"Come in, come in, rest thyself," came Aunt Charity's friendly voice, and before they could all three get inside the door, she had uncovered the plate on the table filled with food ready for Rosetta to eat.

Uncle Jesse did not delay her with a prayer. Rosetta sat in the spot Aunt Charity indicated, picked up her fork, and began to eat in a slow and mannerly way, surprising for someone who had been nearly starved on the road. When she had finished, she sat back and said to Aunt Charity, "Thank you, ma'am. That was mighty good." And though they could not fully see her face—no candles were lit—they could hear the contentment in her voice.

They remained silent for a while. Aunt Charity quietly took Rosetta's plate away and washed it and then sat down next to her at the table. Laura joined her there. Uncle Jesse stood in the shadow of the doorway, and though his body was relaxed, Laura knew that his eyes scanned the horizon for any movement, ears alert to every sound. Finally, as if he felt comfortable enough only then, he questioned Rosetta. "Thou had a long journey, child?"

Rosetta did not answer him at first, her head turned away. Then, cautiously, the words came out. "Oh, I don't know how many days, sir. Mostly I was sleeping when it was light, hid in some haystack, then running at night with only the North Star to show me the way and dogs chasing behind me. I lost count after a while. Maybe a week now. I don't know."

"Why?" Laura asked, and her voice sounded loud in her ears. "Why did you run away?"

Rosetta turned toward her. "Why?" she repeated. "Oh, miss, don't you *know*?"

The moon was up now and Laura could see the girl's eyes, though not their depth, their watery surface unrevealing. She could not answer and sat with her hands folded in her lap as if she sat in church.

Finally Rosetta spoke again. "Sooner or later we all try to get away. Some make it. Some don't. But me, I'd rather be dead than go back there to that old place."

And then Rosetta told them her story, as if it were the one small gift of thanks she could give them for their care.

Chapter Five

Rosetta's Story

It won't so bad at first. Me just a little bitty thing in nothing but a raggedy dress, running around picking up a leaf or flower to show my mama and say, "Ain't that pretty?" And her sighing, answering back, "Lord, chile, I ain't got no time for flowers," but she'd give me a kiss anyway and then go back to work.

My mama was a house nigger. Worked in the big house for Miz Burris from the time she was a little girl. Many a time I hear Miz Burris say, "Eliza, you cook better than me any day. Mr. Burris wouldn't eat a mouthful of my cornbread long as he could get yours." She was a good woman, Christian, never mean like some I heard of. Spill one drop of water from the bucket and get hit upside the head. But not Miz Burris. She'd be smiling when I came to the house looking for Mama, say, "How you, Rosetta?" nice as anything.

Mama didn't like for me to come up there to the house, though. "You go back to the cabins," she'd say when I come running to show her a pretty thing I'd found. "You stay out of trouble." But I wouldn't always do what she said, hid out just to see what was going on. Won't nothing happening at the cabins. Folks had all gone off to the fields or wherever else they worked, nobody around 'cept some other young-uns not much older than me, tending to babies while they mamas was gone. They didn't like me anyway. Jealous. "Thinks she's better," they'd say, "'cause her skin is light yellow, 'cause her mama works at the big house and gets special favors." Won't very special, I could've told them. A little bit of meat every now and then, a piece of cloth left over from a dress Miz Burris was having made that Mama could turn into something for me. And there was plenty others around with light-colored skin.

Night was different. The sun would be setting, and folks would be coming back from the fields, and you could hear a few singing, just light at first, no more'n a buzzing. And though everybody would be dog tired, they'd sit and talk a minute, resting, while the children brushed up against them wanting a hug. Then they'd fix supper, as likely as not all together, everybody bringing what food they had and putting it in the cooking pot.

Mama would dip out enough for me and her with the old china teacup, white with flowers running up, just a tiny chip in it, she'd found up near the house. Lord, I kept that cup for years, the only thing I had from her.

But there'd be better times. Sunday afternoons when nobody had to work and Mr. Burris donated a pig for a barbecue, the men would dig a pit, get the fire going, and when the coals was red hot, put that pig, all tied up on a spit, right over them to cook. People would come to visit from miles around, though they wasn't supposed to without a pass. You could get arrested on the road. But that didn't seem to stop 'em, the men especially, the courting ones. They'd walk all morning to come see them a pretty girl all dressed up and then walk back the whole way again that night in the dark, too tired hardly to lift a hoe next day but worth it.

Children played and played. Some would be strangers, visiting from the next plantation over, and I would gather up the little ones and we'd play school, me the teacher, them the pupils that got yelled at. I could do it good—learned sitting outside the schoolhouse behind a bush. I wasn't supposed to be there, wasn't supposed to learn one thing. It was against the law. But Miz Burris told my mama, "Let her go, won't hurt one thing," so I was able to learn my letters and do some figuring. I can write my name, more'n a lot can do.

But things changed. One day, just like any other it seemed at first, Mama came to the cabin when last light was fading and sat down on the steps. "Eliza, what's wrong with you?" one of the other ladies asked. I looked sharp at her, then back at my mama and felt so bad that I hadn't even stared at her real good, just accepted that she was *there*. Because Mama's face was pulled way down like I'd seen it only once before when my grandmama died and she was hollering with the others at the funeral.

"Lord, have mercy," she said, and started to say more. Then she noticed me standing up beside her. "Rosetta, you get away, mind your own business. We got grown-up talking to do," and she pointed to the end of the house. I walked real slow, but I knew I had to go or else I'd get a whipping later on. Didn't say nothing about how *far* I had to go, so soon as I turned the corner, I just stood there listening to them talk.

"It's Miz Burris," Mama said. "She's real sick. Always was a peaked thing, eat like a bird and stay up in her room a lot. Mr. Burris, he be fussing at her to eat more, get up and go visiting, get her mind off things. But she don't do it, stay shut up in that house with the doctor calling all times of the day and night when she have a spell.

"'Stay with me, Eliza,' she say. 'I'm afraid.' And what could I do 'cept sit there by her bed with night coming on and me with a peck of work to do before I can get home? She be nice to me. 'Take you some of that ham,' she say. 'Lord knows, I can't eat a bite.' So I would slice up a piece or two and take it home for me and Rosetta.

"She's worse now, got the lung trouble, the doctor say, coughs all the time, and I have to change the sheets 'cause of the blood that comes up. Mr. Burris, he walks around the house like he a haint or something, and he grabbed the doctor when he come out of Miz Burris's room and ask him, 'How is she?' But the doctor just shake his head and Mr. Burris go back to walking. About all I can do is cook, but even when I make something special she likes, Miz Burris ain't got no appetite and she can't keep nothing down from coughing. Mr. Burris don't seem to eat a-tall. About the only thing he pour down his throat is a glass of whiskey."

Mama don't say any more, but after that night, each time she come back to the cabin from the house, I'd look and see that her eyes were a little sadder, her body a little tireder, until she finally come one day and told us all that Miz Burris was dead, died in her sleep, peaceful at last. Nobody worked in the fields the next day, and we all went to her funeral. They buried her in the churchyard with all those pretty tombstones around. Later, Mr. Burris put one on her grave.

For a while, things don't change much. We don't see much of Mr. Burris, and I'd overhear Mama say to the ladies, "He hardly ever around. I keep up the house, cook his supper, but he gone half the time or cuddled up with a liquor bottle." If it won't for the overseer nothing would've ever got done. We got used to things staying like they were, and when they changed, it was a surprise to everybody.

Miss Sarah Louise was the change. One day I see Mama coming home lickety-split down the road to the cabins, and I could tell she was about to bust with something. "Guess what?" she say. "Mr. Burris is going to get him a new wife. Already got her picked out, down from Sanderford way. She be *young,* they say. Ain't that always the way? Mens want to get them a young gal if they have a chance the second time around. Maybe Mr. Burris want him some children since Miz Burris never give him any. Lord, I bet things change around here."

We all went to the wedding, same as the funeral, 'cept it won't at the church but on the front porch of the house. Mr. Burris got his cousin to come and take charge, and she spent a week, day and night, getting ready. Ran everybody ragged. "Polish up that silver. Take up that carpet and beat it." She never stopped, but I think my mama didn't mind it. She got a gleam back in her eye, and she stepped livelier on the path when she come home at night.

Finally, we was ready. House shiny as a new toy. Enough food cooked for an army and a barbecue pit dug. All of us handed some extra food, too, and the men a ration of tobacco.

Mr. Burris brought her back on the wagon, Miss Sarah Louise. I was standing on the porch beside Mama, straining my neck to see, when she come riding up pretty as a picture in a ruffly dress and bonnet to match. Hair curled around her face bright as angel wings in a Bible book. Careful, like she might break, Mr. Burris helped her down, and then she traipsed up the path to the door, smiling and smirking to beat the band. Mr. Burris's cousin rushed out the door, crying, "Welcome! Welcome! You come right on in. I know you must be worn out after that ride."

I stayed busy all afternoon, helping Mama up at the house. I was old enough by then, no more playing around the cabins in my petticoat, and I ran back and forth to the kitchen, bringing glasses of lemonade for the ladies in the parlor and whiskey for the men out on the porch. Nobody paid any attention to me, and I could listen to all their talk about Mr. Burris and Miss Sarah Louise. "Got him a young one," somebody would say. "Pretty." And then somebody else would answer with a laugh, "I expect it was more like she got *him*. She probably jumped at the chance to become the new Miz Burris."

The wedding took place the next afternoon. The preacher arrived, all smiles, black as a crow in his preacher's suit, and the yard was full of folks. All around us hung the scent of pig cooking, drowning out the flower smells of the ladies; and the men, hot in Sunday clothes, took off their coats and draped them over the backs of chairs.

Finally it was time. Everybody got real quiet, almost like somebody died, and then the front door opened and there was Mr. Burris, smiling like somebody give him a front row seat in heaven, with Miss Sarah Louise hanging on his arm. Folks cheered then, even whistled, while the two of them walked slowly down the steps to where the preacher stood.

But, my, didn't she look pretty! Miss Sarah Louise all done up in her wedding finery, that gold hair piled up, shimmery white dress dragging on the ground when she walked. She carried a bunch of white roses that grew wild back of the house tied up with a ribbon. When Mr. Burris kissed her, he had to bend over, like she was a little child.

But Miss Sarah Louise didn't act like no baby. A long time after I heard my mama say, "I should of knowed right then, when she come into the kitchen, not one hour married, and started complaining, that she was gonna take over." Before the last guest was out of sight, she was ordering Mama and me around like we didn't have a lick of sense. "We'll talk about your duties in the morning," she said, and then went off to bed. Mama rolled her eyes but didn't say nothing—at least, not then.

But things only went from bad to worse between them. Seemed like nothing Mama did pleased Miss

Sarah Louise. "I don't know what ails that woman," I'd hear her say to Mr. Burris. "I thinks she deliberately tries to get my goat, doing things I tell her not to." I stayed away from her best I could, but still she'd come up to me in the house while I was doing my work and give me a hard look, like she was gonna light in on me and start fussing any minute.

Then another change came. Miss Sarah Louise got in the family way, and for a while we had a little peace. She stayed upstairs most of the time, calling for somebody to bring her a glass of lemonade. I'd take it up to her and she'd be lying up in bed looking at the pattern book, though I could tell her she won't going to be needing no new dresses for a while until that baby come. But at least she was occupied, not snooping 'round the house, and Mama began to sing again while she worked.

When the day come for the birthing, you could've heard Miss Sarah Louise yelling in the next county. Mama helped out the doctor, and she said later that Miss Sarah Louise didn't have it no worse than anybody else, was just spoiled and thought it'd be different for her. All her bossy ways came back, and she started ordering Mama around again. "Change that child," she'd say and hand over the baby to Mama to take care of. I was already sick of boiling stinky diapers in the big iron pot out by the washhouse, and it won't long before Miss Sarah Louise found another chore for me to do.

Mama was cooking dinner and I was with her scraping some new potatoes when Miss Sarah Louise come into the kitchen. The baby was upstairs asleep. "Eliza," she say, not looking at either one of us, "I want Rosetta to start staying up here at the house at night. I can't get up every time that baby cries, and Mr. Burris fusses if he don't get enough sleep."

"What you mean?" my mama asked.

Miss Sarah Louise poked her neck out. You could see it all splotchy and red over her collar. "Just what I said. I want Rosetta to stay in the baby's room at night, rock her if she cries, feed her if need be. She can sleep on the floor beside the cradle."

"She ain't old enough to be taking care of no youngun. She ain't much older'n a baby herself."

Miss Sarah Louise make a motion like she was waving at gnats. "Sure she's old enough." She turned around and marched out of the kitchen and Mama gave her a look that could kill.

But what could she do about it? If she go to Mr. Burris, he ain't going to do nothing, and Miss Sarah Louise already made up her mind. So next night, I ate my supper at home and then went back to the house and climbed upstairs. Mr. Burris won't nowhere around, and Miss Sarah Louise was doing some sewing.

"She's asleep now," she called out to me. "You wait in there for when she wakes," and I laid down on the bare floor and tried to sleep. Later, I woke up when Mr. Burris come home and the baby started to cry so that I had to keep my foot just a-going on the cradle to keep her quiet.

That baby be all right. Lucretia they called it, after somebody's grandmama. That did seem like an awful long name to put on the poor little thing. Because she won't pretty, pale as milk with no hair, and a rash over her body when it was hot. She cried and cried sometimes, and nothing would stop her no matter how fast I rocked. I didn't get much sleep, and I'd drag around during the day, nearly falling off my chair if I sat down.

"That's enough," Mama finally said. "You are going to sleep right here in this kitchen," and she made me a pallet at the back of the pantry, dark there, cool most days, with roses running over the window outside and the smell of dried apples hanging in the air.

"What if Miss Sarah Louise catches me?" I asked her.

"Lord, chile, you ever see her in this kitchen when I'm around? She stay away like it's the front door where the devil lives. You go ahead and rest and let me worry 'bout Miss Sarah Louise."

So I began to sleep there in the pantry during the afternoon, the house quiet 'cept for Mama when she sang, and the house squeaking every now and then. If I didn't sleep at night, it won't no matter. I even got so I liked to play with little Lucretia, like she was my own baby doll.

'Course it don't last. One day I was sound asleep when the pantry door cracked open. Miss Sarah Louise was standing there. "What are you doing?" she asked me. "You lazing around in here while there's work to do? You lazy nigger, get on out of there," and she reached in and took me by the hair and pulled me out of the pantry.

I yelled, couldn't help it my head hurt so, and Mama was right there mad as a hornet. "You don't hurt my chile," she said to Miss Sarah Louise. "You take your hand off her this minute."

Miss Sarah Louise let go, drew back, and put her hand on the little dangley watch she wears on her chest. "How dare you talk to me like that?" she said, just a-quivering. "I ought to have you beat." But she went on out and we heard her climbing the stairs, and she didn't come down the rest of the day.

No surprise, Miss Sarah Louise told Mr. Burris that very night. "That woman makes me afraid," she told him after he came to bed. I kept the cradle going fast as I could, hoping the baby wouldn't holler. "She could of raised up a frying pan and hit me over the head. I'm alone here in this house all day long with her and that no-count daughter of hers, no telling what they might do. You've got to do something. Anybody else, they'd beat her half to death. I won't breathe a safe breath till she's gone."

I didn't tell Mama what I heard, kept it to myself like a hurt bandaged up in secret. But when nothing happened the next day and then the next, I began to think, *Maybe it all is going to blow over. Miss Sarah Louise just in a pout. It ain't the first time and won't be the last.*

But I was wrong, because two days later, Mr. Burris called Mama to his office and, in no more'n two minutes and hardly that many more words, changed all our lives.

It was sunshiny that day, a little cooler. I was shelling butter beans out on the back porch, ready to cook for dinner. Mama was upstairs changing beds. The only thing different was that Mr. Burris had stayed in his office at the house after breakfast 'stead of going to the fields till he came out and called upstairs for Mama to come down. Miss Sarah Louise was nowhere to be seen.

I still didn't think nothing about it, sitting there like a fool with butter beans in my lap and my mind stuck on some crazy notion like I was going to get me a new ribbon for my hair. Then it came, a sound like somebody dying rushing through Mr. Burris's door faster than wind. I jumped up. The butter beans went flying. And then Mama came through the door, eyes streaming and blind to me, mouth still open in a wail, and ran right past.

"Mama!" I cried out, but she don't hear me, so I take out after her, running barefoot through weeds and rocks down to the path that led to the cabins. She just dropped there, like she'd lost all her breath and had nothing left and would never get it back again. "Mama!" I said, and throwed myself on top of her, felt her jerky breathing and knew she was alive.

Finally she raised up her head. Tears still ran from her eyes. When she spoke, it was like somebody else's voice, a stranger I'd never heard before. "Oh, my baby chile," she said, and grabbed me to her; and then I began to cry, too, not even knowing yet what had happened, just scared. For I don't know how long we sat there holding each other, till the tears finally stopped and Mama got her breath back and she said in that strange voice, "He gonna sell me, gonna send me away from this place for good."

I couldn't think what those words meant at first. I knew that others got sent away to be sold. People'd laugh and say, "Mr. Burris gonna spend all his money on that fancy wife of his, have to sell some of us folks," but it seemed like a joke. "Me too?" I asked Mama, never thinking it would be any different. Mama didn't answer, just pulled me close again so that I could feel her heart bumping in her chest like it was something being chased.

She never did say in words, *I be leaving you,* but I watched her each day as she packed up what few things she had, going around to others to give them what she didn't need anymore—a dish, a spoon. "I guess whoever I go to will at least have a bowl for me to eat out of. You take this," she'd say. In the night we would lie side by side on the bed, both of us wide awake, but still there would be no words. And no touching, either, as if Mama had cut off her hands on purpose, ready for when she could hold me close no longer.

They left at dawn one day. Four of 'em besides my mama setting up on the wagon, along with other goods Mr. Burris was sending to market. The overseer was driving them there. "Well," he said in a voice almost kindly, "we might as well get on our way, 'fore it gets too hot." He allowed us a little time to say good-bye. Others were crying, holding on to each other, and when Mama did finally hug me, I could feel her tremble all over. "You be a good chile. I be back," she whispered in my ear. And with that, she climbed up into the wagon and took a seat and never looked around again as they drove away.

"Mama!" I yelled out once and started to run after the wagon, but some ladies held me back, saying, "Hush now, it won't do no good. She's gone." I fell to the ground, feeling like my heart had been tore out by the roots, and I was sick for three days—didn't sleep, didn't eat a mouthful, just sat inside the dark cabin. Even that I had to move out of. Others took it over, and I went to live with an old granny too sick to work and needing help.

I didn't last long up at the house after that. I didn't care much about anything. Burned whatever I tried to cook, scratched up furniture, broke glasses. Miss Sarah Louise yelled, but she didn't lay a hand on me. Mr. Burris was never around. Folks said he drank a lot, went to cockfights out in the woods, and a few times I heard them fussing upstairs in their bedroom.

Miss Sarah Louise didn't have the nerve to tell me to my face. The woman who'd replaced Mama in the house told me. "They don't want you working here anymore. You going to have to work the fields."

"That's just fine with me," I said, and marched out of the house and went to sit in the woods where it was cool the rest of the afternoon. Next morning I was up at the first sound of the overseer's horn and went off to the cotton field and took up my bag like everybody else.

It was hard work, whoo-ee. Hot sun shining down on your head and back about to break. By nightfall my fingers pure bled from the scratchy brown stems of the cotton bolls, and my feet was burnt from standing on hot stones.

But it won't all bad. I won't the only young-un working the fields, and when it was time to eat, we'd go off by ourselves and stretch out under a tree for a rest, sharing what little we had. We laughed and talked about whatever was going on, sometimes in whispers about others who'd got away and how. That was like dreaming to me, to think I might leave someday, too, but I listened carefully and put away what was said in the back of my mind.

So time passed on. The hurt in my heart where Mama was torn away healed over, and though the scab got pulled off again sometimes, it didn't pain me so, and

I had a space there for somebody else. Who? His name was Samson, like the man in the Bible that tore the temple down.

We met at a Sunday afternoon barbecue, him come over with others from the next plantation. When I first saw him, he was standing off by hisself next to a China tree with his arms folded across his chest like he had to protect hisself from something. Girls gave him the eye, but he didn't bother none with them. He looked strong as the man in the Bible, good-looking, too, skin like copper—his daddy was part Indian—and I never thought he'd take any notice of me. But the others began to tease, "Rosetta, that Samson, he be liking you, watch you all the time." And I'd answer back, "Naw he ain't, he just stuck-up, thinks he's better'n the rest of us."

But then, I started to think maybe they was right. Every Sunday, barbecue or not, he began to show up, still staying off to hisself, and I could feel his eyes like hot breath on the back of my neck. Finally I thought, *Well, mister, we'll just see who you're after,* and I marched right over to him, China tree berries cracking under my feet like gunshot, and said, "How do? I'm Rosetta. What's your name?"

Well, you shoulda seen him, turned redder than his Indian pappy, and I knew right then he was just shy, not stuck-up a-tall.

"They call me Samson," he said, but he wouldn't look at me, eyes down to his feet in them big shoes that had no ties.

"You from around here?" I asked, knowing already that he was.

"Down thataway," he said, and bent his head toward the trees.

"That's not a very far piece," I said, and he nodded.

We talked on. Ask me now what about and I couldn't tell you one thing. And even though he started coming to see me every Sunday regular as clockwork, we still didn't talk personal for a long time. It was hard for me to talk about my mama, open up the hurt in my heart; and he hurt, too, but more on the outside where he got whupped by the overseer. "One day I kill him," Samson said to me, and I got a chill all over and tol' him to hush before somebody heard.

Won't no surprise when he finally asked me to marry him. 'Sure enough," I said before he could bat an eye. Then he hugged me for all to see, face turning red again, and there won't no need to tell anybody what was going on.

We was married in the spring. Down by the orchard where the trees were blooming white as clouds, petals dropping if you just touched a branch. An old man they called Preacher said the words, and it didn't matter whether they were the right ones or not, we knew we was blessed in God's sight.

Oh, you should've seen me, got up so I hardly knew myself when I looked in a piece of mirror. The others lent me things, a belt with a sparkly buckle, ribbons to do up my hair, a blouse with big puffed sleeves. And Samson was dressed up, too, with a full suit on, somebody else's—tight as skin on him, he be so big.

It was a happy time, a pig on the spit and cakes and pies on a loaded-down table, and dancing when it started to get dark. They must of heard us up at the big house, but nobody come to holler. Samson and I sat close, him shy again but happy, I could tell. And my own sorrow seemed far away then, like an echo that could hardly be heard. Then it was time to go. Daylight would be coming in a few hours and Samson would be missed if he won't there. "I'll sneak off a night soon," he whispered as he kissed me. "You leave the door open." And he was gone off into the dark.

Not much changed after that. It was still almost like we was courting, Samson there every Sunday, walking all those miles in and out of trees so he wouldn't be seen, then slipping back again at nightfall. And for a while we didn't mind. We was in love and nothing else mattered. But then I'd see Samson coming down the road, head down before he'd seen me, and I could tell by the way he walked and the look on his face that he won't happy.

He didn't talk about the beatings he got, but I could see the bruises even in the dark night. I could feel the anger in him like a fever on his skin. Finally he told me about the man.

"He a slave, too," Samson said, his eyes all lit up, "or was, 'fore he got away. Now he come back to help others. He say it ain't all that hard. All sorts of folks'll help—white folks, even, that think it be wrong to own slaves. They'll hide you, give you food, send you on to the next place. You have to trust. 'Follow the North Star,' he say, 'and you'll make it.'"

"How you know he ain't fooling?" I ask him. "You heard about others, taking what little money they have and paying it out to some scallywag that says he can get 'em away, then turns them in to the white man for a reward. It'd be twice as bad when you come back."

"Naw," he answered back to me. "Nothing like that. This man be *good*, you can tell. He a preacher man now, say he doing it for the Lord."

What else could I say? I didn't know more'n Samson whether that man was good or bad, but I loved Samson and was ready to do whatever he said. Things mighta gone on the same there at Mr. Burris's place and Samson coulda gone on surviving the bruises, but who knew when things might change? "All right," I told him finally. "You talk to the man. Tell me what to do," and he hugged me so hard I thought I'd break half in two.

"We'll be free and happy someday soon," he said, "no more worries about being beat or going hungry." And my mind rested after that. I believed Samson, believed the slave man I never even seen, that it was all going to turn out right. Even began to think that maybe some white folks could be trusted.

We waited some days till the moon was just a sliver so it wouldn't be so bright, though the stars still shone down to guide us. We was to go separate, me one way, Samson another. He told me how to find the first place where I could get help, what signs to watch for, said they'd show me the next way, then we'd meet up. I tried not to think about being out in the woods by myself in the dark, no telling what might be under foot. I won't supposed to take much with me, just a little food and my shoes. "Can I take my mama's pretty cup? It's the only thing I got of hers," I said. But he answered me, "Naw, leave it behind. It'll only get broke."

I didn't say bye to no one. Samson said not to, it'd be safer if people could say in truth they hadn't seen hide nor hair of me since the day before. I slipped out of the cabin and walked down the path to the road in front of the house, stopping only once to look back at that big old place where I'd spent all my life so far. I didn't feel no sadness over leaving. Mama was gone. Samson was waiting for me up ahead. What did I have to keep me there on the plantation 'cept a lot of hard work and worse to be expected?

I won't tell you much about the next few days. I scrambled through the woods at night. When my food gave out, I pulled apples off trees and picked berries, and once I milked a cow, sneaking up to a barn. Worst thing, though, was the dogs howling, sometimes real close, and I'd stumble and think they'd be on me soon. But I did what Samson had told me to, found a creek and walked up the middle so the dogs would lose the scent, and went on.

Finally I made it to the place we was to meet. They was an old couple, had been slaves but their master, when he died, set them free and gave them a piece of land. They hid me in a space so little it made me think I was in my coffin, but I tried not to think about that, kept only Samson and the end of our journey on my mind.

But he didn't come! One day went by, two, and I could tell the old folks was getting nervous. "It happens," they said. "Folks get lost, get chased out of the way. You'd better go on. There's another place to hide down the road. Maybe he's there already, this Samson. You better go see."

I left that night, with a little more food and nothing else, not even the hope I'd see Samson in a day or two. Somehow I knew he won't going to be at the next stop. I didn't know what had happened but I could feel something bad in my bones.

I traveled days more, no chance to rest. When they told me about this place, I thought, *It may be the last.* But I kept traveling, found the creek, climbed up the bank by the tree with a notch on it I'd been told about and stepped into the tunnel. Lord, I thought again I was being buried, and when you all found me down beneath the meat house I just knew it was the end. I'd die there and become a pile of bones. 'Stead, you've been good to me, not like any white folks I ever met before. I praise the Lord.

But what happens now? Where's Samson? What am I gonna do?

Chapter Six

A Secret Revealed

It was very late when Rosetta stopped speaking. The moon had dipped away, the stars had paled. Beneath the porch Ninevah made little whimpers, lost in dreams. No one spoke in the room. Uncle Jesse still stood in the doorway, smoke drifting from his pipe in wispy clouds, while Aunt Charity and Laura sat at the table, hands folded in their laps. Rosetta might have been asleep, her head on her arms on the table.

Finally Aunt Charity broke the silence. "We must get thee to bed," she said, patting Rosetta on the arm. She turned to Laura. "Thee as well. It has been a long day for all. The rooster will be crowing before we know it."

Uncle Jesse turned, silhouetted by the light. Laura could not see his eyes. "I will take thee back to the meat house," he said. "There is no one about."

Laura could feel Rosetta shudder beside her. "Can't she stay here in the house?" she asked. "Nobody will know."

"It's not safe," Uncle Jesse answered. He turned toward Rosetta. "I hate to put thee back in that hole," he told her, "but it's the best we can do for now. We'll get thee away soon." He walked outside and knocked the ashes from his pipe on the porch railing. Beneath him Ninevah gave a low growl but then was quiet.

"I'll go," Rosetta said, pushing herself up slowly from the table. "It ain't so bad out there, not like sleeping in the woods or in somebody's haystack." She turned and the light caught her, and Laura saw again her bare arms, the ragged dress. Her heart jumped. What if *she* were the one returning to that dark hole, the echo of howling dogs always in her ears? How would she feel? She must do something to ease Rosetta's pain.

"Wait," she said. "Come upstairs with me. I want to see something." And before Aunt Charity or Uncle Jesse could object, she took a candle, grabbed Rosetta's hand, and pulled her up the stairs.

"Well, mercy me," Aunt Charity said, but Laura closed the door and heard nothing more.

"You can wear my dress," Laura said to Rosetta,

going to the washstand. She bent, pulled open the doors and reached inside. "Here," she said, taking out the dress she had worn that afternoon and then hidden away. The skirt was torn and dusty around the hem, and the cuffs were stained, but it would cover Rosetta better than the rags she was wearing.

"Oh, no, miss," Rosetta said, pulling back. "I can't do that."

"Yes, you can." She reached to the rear of the washstand and got out some of the clean white underwear Nellie had ironed for her just a few nights before. *What if Mama knew I was giving it to some escaped slave girl?* she thought. *How shocked she would be!* She almost laughed out loud. "You can wash," she said to Rosetta, pointing to the porcelain bowl and pitcher on top of the stand.

Rosetta took the dress, holding it gently. Her eyes had lost some of their wariness. Laura turned and looked out the window while Rosetta splashed at the washstand. Aunt Charity's muffled voice called up once, but Laura didn't answer her.

"All right, miss, I'm ready." Rosetta still sounded hesitant. Slowly Laura turned, and when she saw Rosetta standing in the middle of the room in the candlelight, she caught her breath.

"Well, aren't you pretty!" she said, trying not to let the surprise sound in her voice. Except for being an inch too short and a little tight in the waist, the dress fit

Rosetta perfectly. Above the collar her pale skin glowed from her bath, and her hair, still uncombed, fell in dark curls down her back. She could be any pretty girl, no hint of slave about her.

"Laura, thou must *hurry*." This time it was Uncle Jesse's voice that called up the stairs, a sense of urgency in his tone.

Laura answered him. "Yes, we're coming," and she took Rosetta's hand and led her down the stairs. At the bottom she paused, waiting for their reaction.

Uncle Jesse and Aunt Charity peered through the gloom. "My goodness," Aunt Charity said. "So *that's* what thou was up to in thy room." She bent closer. "Thine own clothes, the ones thou wore today." She smiled. "How kind." She might have said more, but Uncle Jesse spoke again.

"We must go. Pretty clothes won't do her any good if she gets caught. It's not long before dawn."

His voice was like a sudden chill in the room. Aunt Charity bustled about, wrapping up a piece of bread and meat in a cloth for Rosetta to take. Laura hurried her to the door. And Uncle Jesse, scanning the horizon once again, led her outside. "Night, ma'am. Night, miss," Rosetta said, touching the bodice of the dress. "Thank you all for everything." Ninevah crawled from beneath the house, stretched, and followed Uncle Jesse and Rosetta as they hastened across the yard.

For a minute or two Laura and Aunt Charity stood silently in the doorway. Then Aunt Charity sighed. "I do hate to see that girl go back to the room beneath the meat house. Poor thing, she's been through enough already."

"Couldn't she stay here at the house?" Laura asked once again. "She could sleep in my room. We could make a pallet on the floor."

Aunt Charity shook her head and turned, and Laura followed her back inside. "It's too dangerous," Aunt Charity said, putting the supper dishes, dry now, back into the cupboard. "Anyone might ride up. People are suspicious, of Quakers in particular. After Jesse freed the slaves here, next time we went to town somebody said right in our hearing, '*His* niggers are going to spoil *our* niggers. What are we going to do about it?' For some, it's been worse, pulled naked from their beds, hot tar poured over them, covered in turkey feathers. Some of our brethren have given up and sold out and moved away."

"Why do you do it?"

Aunt Charity leaned against the table. "Ah, that," she said. "It is God's calling. We must seek to help others, reveal the light within them."

"How? What happens next? Where will Rosetta go?"

Aunt Charity did not answer at once. "We're not sure," she finally said. "Jesse has sent out word. We are waiting to hear from someone who can help."

"But you can't just turn her out by herself."

"We may have to. We may have no other choice. But pray to God that it isn't so."

Uncle Jesse's foot hit the first step outside. Then his shadow filled the doorway. "She's abed," he said. "Safe for now. It's time for the rest of us to get some sleep. Morning will come soon enough. Go on up, Laura. Thou has had a long day."

Laura didn't argue but said good night to both of them, then went up to her room. Pulling off her dress, she hung it on the back of the door and went to stand again by the window. Nothing in her view had changed. The crape myrtles still stood there ruffled in the starlight, the white sand glowed. Down by the road the oak tree shed dark shadows, and she pictured the hens in the henhouse swelling their feathers, waiting for the rooster's cry. But she knew that, farther in the darkness, Rosetta lay on her bed of hay, alone, with only a sputtering candle for company, waiting for Lord knows what, already with enough hurt in her heart to last a lifetime. Laura had only glimpsed such things from afar, able to ignore what did not please her. Till now, she had stayed that little child hiding her head under pillows, trying to blot out the sound of shots at hog-killing time. She had seen men and women working in the fields but had turned away from their sweat and bleeding hands. She had seen the whip on Mr. Hawes's saddle but told herself he would never hit them, it was only to flick flies from the horse's mane. When the preacher said in church that there was no more harm in separating a slave family than a litter of pigs, she never questioned his words.

But what could she do? She had given her dress to Rosetta, but how small a gift that was. The only money she had was the coins her papa had given her for treats on her trip. Maybe if she prayed, God would tell her what to do. She was about to drop on her knees when she heard voices downstairs, Aunt Charity and Uncle Jesse still awake in the kitchen. As she moved across the floor, her prayer became, *Don't let them hear me!* and she stood listening by the door.

"Is she all right?" Aunt Charity said.

"Yes, settled, I think. She has nothing to be frightened of right now." Uncle Jesse sounded tired.

"What will we do with her?"

There was silence for a moment. Then Uncle Jesse said, "Send her on. What else? Thou knows as well as I."

Laura heard Aunt Charity give a little cry. "Oh, but she is so young, so defenseless. How can we send her back to the woods with just a few days' rations? Nothing to guide her except the North Star?"

"Thou forgets. She has come this far on her own, clambered through streams to avoid the dogs, hidden in haystacks. She is strong, that girl."

"There is still hope?"

"Yes, of course. We may receive word that someone ahead can take her. But it is a bad time. Slave catchers are on the roads. Dogs roam at night. Few can be trusted."

"I will pray we find a way. It must be soon. She cannot go on alone too long."

Aunt Charity's voice was strong, like a command. Uncle Jesse sounded almost angry when he answered her. "Why is this one so different?" he asked. "We have had others before her sleeping beneath the meat house. Hers is not the first sad story thou has heard."

Though she was upstairs, behind a cracked door, Laura could feel the tension in the room below. "She *is* different," Aunt Charity said at last. "She is not like the others."

"Thou must tell me. I do not know." The anger was still there. Again there was silence. Laura pressed her ear closer to the door.

"She is with child," Aunt Charity finally said. "She is going to have a baby. She needs good food, rest, someone to help her when the time comes. We must get her away to freedom before that day. For her own sake, for the baby's."

Laura fell back. She did not hear more. Rosetta was going to have a baby! No wonder the dress had been tight in the waist. She should have known. But Rosetta's rags had hung loosely, and Laura had been too excited dressing her up like a doll to think about the swelling of her belly. Not surprising that Aunt Charity was concerned. They couldn't just send Rosetta off into the woods to follow a star. They would have to come up with some other plan. But what? She stood in the middle of the floor, feeling lost.

The rooster crowed. Soon it would be dawn. Laura knelt and began to pray. "Dear Jesus, please help us find a way to save Rosetta and her baby. You must know what she has been through. Please pity her. Show us what to do."

She opened her eyes. The pale light coming through the window had brightened, bringing to life the twining pattern of tiny blue and pink flowers on her dress hanging on the back of the door. She thought again of Rosetta, sleeping beneath the meat house in her castoff clothes, of the child inside her.

And then she knew. As real as if someone had picked a piece of fruit from a tree and handed it to her to eat, the idea came to her. She knew how they could save Rosetta and her child. "Thank you," she said aloud, and then hurried to her bed for sleep.

Chapter Seven

Laura's Plan

"Thou cannot do it. What would thy mama and papa think of me? No. Put it out of thy mind right this minute. I won't hear of it."

Aunt Charity, shaking her head, went over to the fireplace, took down a kettle of hot water, and walked back to the counter where she was working butter into molds. She and Uncle Jesse had long ago finished breakfast, but Laura, oversleeping again, had come down late. Before she could eat even one bite of the food Aunt Charity set out before her, she had blurted out her plan. "Why not?" she asked, picking up a piece of bacon. At home her mother would have told her it was impolite to use her fingers.

"Because it is dangerous. I have told thee what can happen. It is not play."

"And I am not a child." Laura's words sounded very loud in the small room. She hoped Aunt Charity wouldn't think her impudent.

Aunt Charity's face softened. "No," she said. "Thou are growing up, plain to see. But it would be too dangerous even for a full-grown woman. Surely thou must understand."

Yes, she thought, *I do understand.* Suddenly she thought of Henry, who tried to act so big and grown-up—wouldn't he be surprised if he knew! She'd show him. She pushed her porridge around in the bowl a few more times, then said again to Aunt Charity's back, "Can't I just *ask* Uncle Jesse? Please!"

Aunt Charity stopped her work. Sighing, with her shoulders slightly stooped, she said without looking around, "Thou never would take no for an answer. Just like thy mama, always must have thy way. All right. Thou can ask thy uncle Jesse. But mark my words, he will say the very same thing."

Laura finished her breakfast. Aunt Charity worked at the counter, slapping the freshly churned pale yellow butter to squeeze out the last bit of water, smoothing it into the molds. The cool sour scent filled the air, and any other time Laura might have asked for a slab to put on her bread. But she did not want to rile Aunt Charity any further, and she remained quiet.

They heard Ninevah long before Uncle Jesse's foot hit the steps of the porch. Laura, finished now, got up from the table, washed her bowl and spoon, then went outside to draw a bucket of water from the well. "Here," she said to Ninevah. "You shouldn't be running around in this heat. Your tongue is dripping." She put down a bowl of fresh water, and the dog began to lap it up. "Would you like a cup?" she asked Uncle Jesse. "It's cool."

"Don't mind if I do." He reached for the dipper Laura held out to him. "Another hot one," he said, and took a drink. "I was clearing brush when I saw Ninevah lying under a piece of shade, and I said to him, 'Dog, thou are smarter than thy master, lying there in the cool. Let us go back to the house. I need to rest out of the sun.' " He sat on the top step, and Ninevah flopped down beside him.

"I'm glad you came back," Laura said. "I have something to ask you."

"What?" he asked. He pulled his pipe from his pocket, tapped it on the edge of the porch, but didn't light it.

"It's about Rosetta."

Uncle Jesse gestured toward the barn with his pipe. "She is all right this morning. I took her some breakfast. She will sleep."

"Ah, not so fast." Aunt Charity appeared in the doorway, drying her hands on her apron. "Thou are a clever girl, Laura, trying to get thy uncle alone to make thy plea." She came outside and sat down. "I will hear it again, if thou please."

Laura walked back and forth between them, too excited to sit down. Ninevah's eyes followed her, as if he expected her to go dashing across the yard for a game of chase. She spoke quickly, body bent slightly forward, hands gesturing to emphasize her words. Not until she finished her plea would she give Uncle Jesse or Aunt Charity a chance to speak.

"I thought of it last night, my plan, before I went to sleep. I wanted to help Rosetta, wanted to do more than just exchange my dress for her old things, but I didn't know how at first. Then I saw my dress hanging on the back of the door, and an idea came into my head of what we can do.

"Rosetta can't go on running through the woods. She needs food and rest. How much longer can you keep her here? What if she lost the baby?"

Aunt Charity had been tapping her foot gently against the rough floorboards of the porch. Now she stopped. "How did thou know about the child? I did not tell thee."

Laura felt her face turn red. "I heard the two of you talking last night. I really didn't mean to listen, but your voices came through the door."

"Thou would have done no such thing at home. Thy mama will say we have led thee astray."

Uncle Jesse shifted, put his pipe back into his shirt pocket. "It makes no difference now. Let her go on. What is thy plan?"

Laura began again, slower this time. She stopped her pacing. "We have to get Rosetta far from here, where she'll be safe and have somebody to take care of her. I can do it. I can take her north and nobody will be suspicious." She lowered her voice. "Rosetta can wear my clothes. She has on my dress right now. Well, we could dress her up and pretend she's my sister. Her skin is light. With a bonnet and gloves on, she can pass. We'll say she's sick, going off up North to see a doctor, too weak even to talk. I'm going along to help her. Our parents can't come because of the harvest. It would work. I know it would. Please, Uncle Jesse, let me do it."

For a long while he was silent. Ninevah sat up and nudged his feet, and he reached down to scratch the back of the dog's neck. Then he spoke. "This is not a game, Laura. People are hurt, killed even, trying to help slaves escape. We cannot send thee out to such danger. Thy parents would never forgive us. We must find another way."

Laura moved closer to him. "I know, Uncle Jesse. I'm not a child anymore. But it's something I *have* to do. My mama and papa don't have to know. Henry isn't coming back for me for weeks. In that time, I can go and come back and no one will ever know."

"That would be deceitful. *We* would know, and thou. How could I ever face them again?" Aunt Charity's voice was sad.

"Sometimes, don't you have to do one bad thing so that a better thing can happen? Mama and Papa would be mad, but Rosetta would be safe. Isn't that more important? Wouldn't God forgive a little lie?"

"Ah, thou would argue down the devil," Aunt Charity said, shaking her head. "I cannot say more about it."

Uncle Jesse turned toward Laura. Ninevah flipped over on his back so that Uncle Jesse could scratch his belly. "It might be possible," he said slowly, avoiding Aunt Charity's eyes, though his words were directed to her. "Ebenezer can drive them in the wagon to Savannah, with Rosetta hidden away. From there they can take the steamer to Charleston and on to Philadelphia. Rosetta would be safe in the city. And the child."

Laura reached over and touched Aunt Charity's sleeve. "It will be all right," she said. "Think about it, Aunt Charity, please. It's the only way."

Aunt Charity didn't answer, just stood up and shook out her skirt. "I have work to do," she said, and went toward the door. There were tears in her eyes. She let the door slam behind her.

Uncle Jesse sighed. "Leave her alone," he said. "She will pray and I will abide by her will. She loves thee. We both do. Thou are like our own child. We could not bear it if something happened to thee. So wait. The Lord will have His way."

He got up then and went into the house. Ninevah stretched, his tail wagging, but Laura did not accept the invitation to scratch him more. Instead she stood up and walked out across the yard to stand beneath the crape myrtles. Ninevah reluctantly followed. "You silly dog," she said, and reached down to pet him. "*You* would let me go, wouldn't you? Maybe you could even come along and protect us." He jumped up, teeth bared as if smiling, and she laughed at him. Looking up through the ruffled flowers, she saw the bright sky glowing, and her heart lifted. It would be all right now. She knew. She would help Rosetta get away. The baby would be safe.

Much later, after Uncle Jesse had called from the back porch to tell her that dinner was ready and she had come inside to sit at the kitchen table, Aunt Charity's words made her decision clear. "And, dear Lord," she said after she had blessed the food, "we pray for Thy children, Laura and Rosetta. Keep them safe on this journey. Let no harm come to them. We put them in Thy care."

Chapter Eight

Getting Ready

Once Aunt Charity had agreed to the idea that Laura and Rosetta would travel north together, she started making plans before they had even finished dinner.

"Thou will leave here with Ebenezer on the wagon, early, before light, though thou will find others on the road, like thee, on the way to market. Rosetta will have to be hidden when she leaves here. The neighbors may have seen thee arrive and won't take any notice of thee, but they haven't seen *two* visitors and will be curious if they see another leaving. Once thou are away, she can come out of hiding and change into thy clothes.

"Of course, we'll have to do some altering. Thy dresses will fit her most places, but the waists have to be let out. We'll do that, Laura, thee and I. Tonight we'll bring Rosetta up to the house once again and have her try on the clothes. Once she gets dressed up, no one will know she's not just a young lady with lung problems going to see a special doctor up North.

"But thou will have to be careful. Laura, thou will do all the talking. Thy 'sister' will be too weak to speak. Thou will have to buy tickets, sign thy names if it is required. Rosetta says she can write her name, but if it is slow and labored, someone might notice. Keep thyselves away from others as much as possible. It's a good idea anyway when traveling. There will be rough people on the road, men of doubtful morals, but they will leave two ladies be if they look respectable and turn away at a coarse remark."

Night came, star-filled, and Uncle Jesse walked out across the yard to the barn and brought Rosetta from the meat house. "Eat thy supper," Aunt Charity said to Rosetta. "Thou will need all thy strength. Tell her what we have planned, Jesse. Come, Laura, we have things to do upstairs."

Laura followed Aunt Charity up the narrow staircase to her room. Aunt Charity carefully set her candle on the floor, then went over and knelt beside Laura's bed. Reaching beneath it, she pulled out a wooden box and slid off the lid. "This will do," she said, and unfolded a brightly patterned quilt. "If the cold can't get through it, I guess the light won't, either."

While Laura held the quilt over the window, Aunt Charity took two nails from her pocket, slipped off her shoe, and tapped the nails through the fabric into the window frame. "There," she said, standing back, a little out of breath. "That should do." Laura let go of the quilt, and it cascaded down, covering the window with a garden of fantastical flowers. They tucked the fabric closely around the window so that light would not seep through, then lit several more candles around the room. Rolling up her sleeves, Aunt Charity walked over to the door and called downstairs. "Are thou finished? Rosetta, thou are needed here."

There was silence for a moment, then the low rumble of Uncle Jesse's voice, and finally the swish of Rosetta's skirts on the stairs. "The Lord bless you, ma'am," she said as she rushed into the room. "You, too, miss," she said to Laura. "The gentleman told me what you-all are planning to do to help me and my baby. You plumb saved our lives. How can I ever make it up to you?"

"No need for that," Aunt Charity said briskly. "It's our bounden duty to help. And thou must learn to call us by our rightful names. I am thine aunt Charity. Laura is thy sister. Call her that. Now take off thy dress so we can fit thee into Laura's clothes."

Rosetta turned and began to pull the dress over her head. Laura spoke. "*She* needs a new name. We can't go on calling her Rosetta. They'll be looking for her by that name."

Aunt Charity paused. Her face glowed moist in the candlelight. When she spoke, her voice was very soft. "We will call her Charlotte," she said. "For my child that was lost."

"What? What do you mean, Aunt Charity?"

"Thou never knew, child. It was when thou was just a babe in arms thyself. I had a child, Charlotte, pretty as a picture. But an epidemic came and took her away, and I never had another. That's why thou are so dear to us, to thy uncle Jesse and me, like our own, and sometimes I think, *This is what my child would have looked like grown up. Laura is the very image of her.*"

No one spoke. A candle sputtered, flared. Finally Aunt Charity said, "Enough of old times gone. We have to think of tomorrow, of Rosetta's—Charlotte's—baby to come. Rosetta will bear that name."

They worked quickly after that. Laura took down her dress from the back of the door and pulled another, still folded, from her trunk. Rosetta put them on and stood trembling with excitement while Aunt Charity measured and pinned the fabric. "Yes, we can let out the seams, drape this just a little bit more. She's not showing that much yet. No one will ever know." But when Laura took down the hat boxes from the top of her wardrobe, Aunt Charity said, "No, it's too late to look at bonnets.

We will have a lot of sewing to do tomorrow. Thou must have thy sleep tonight."

They hung up the dresses, closed the trunks. After Laura had put out the candles, Aunt Charity took the quilt down from the window. Cool air blew in, almost chilling. Rosetta quickly pulled on her clothes. "Come," Aunt Charity said, leading her to the doorway. "A few more nights beneath the earth and thou will be gone, free."

"Oh, I can bear it," Rosetta said. "Now I know you-all are going to help me, I got some hope again."

Next morning, right after breakfast, Aunt Charity began to sew. "Here," she said to Laura, handing her a small pair of scissors from her workbasket, "pick out those stitches." She pointed to the dress Laura had brought down from her room. "We'll let it out in the waist—the seams are plentiful—and there will be enough room. Nellie did a good job of sewing. Thy mother has been lucky to have her all these years."

Laura began to snip the tiny stitches. Only a week before she had stood in that dress back home in the upstairs bedroom they used for sewing. "You stand still," Nellie had told her sharply. "If this hem come out wavy, your mama gonna fuss from now to kingdom come. She want you looking *pretty* when you be visiting Miss Charity, Mr. Jesse. Don't you fret."

Impatient, Laura had looked down at the tiers of ruffles that made the skirt of the dress. "I won't need any fancy clothes there, Nellie. You know that. They don't have singing parties in the evening or go around drinking tea in the afternoon. The only time ladies dress up is for Sunday meeting, and even then it's plain as plain can be. I'll stick out like some heathen."

"Don't you mind," said Nellie, her lips pursed around pins. "You just might meet you a young gentleman. Then you'll be glad you got you a nice dress on."

"*Nellie!*" she had said, and turned so that her petticoats flounced around. Nellie just laughed and kept on pinning up the hem.

Laura and Aunt Charity worked through dinnertime. Uncle Jesse came back to the house, found a cold piece of cornbread left over from the day before, and ate it along with a cup of buttermilk and an early apple he had pulled from the branches of the orchard. "Thee are powerful busy," he said, laughing, "and a poor man gets nothing to eat but cold bread."

Aunt Charity sniffed. "God gave thee two hands," she said. "Use them. We must finish these dresses while the light is still good. Thou has thy own work to do. Do it. That poor girl went without hot food for days. Surely thou can stand it for one."

Still laughing, Uncle Jesse opened the door and went outside.

They continued on into the afternoon, stopping only once to eat a piece of bread spread with molasses. It was quiet in the room, though they could hear the buzz of insects beneath the window. Outside, the sun was a pale yellow blur, the blue washed out of the sky as from faded clothes. Laura loosened the neck of her dress but felt no cooler. They began working on the second dress, the one that had hung on the back of Laura's door, with the pattern of pink and blue flowers. Nellie had made that dress, too.

At first they paid no attention to Ninevah's barking. He'd treed a squirrel, perhaps, or chased Uncle Jesse in some silly game. But then the barks became louder, more insistent, and when Laura and Aunt Charity both stood up and went to the doorway, they heard hoofbeats coming down the road. "Dear Lord," Aunt Charity said, her fingers fluttering at her throat. "Who can that be?" She opened the door and looked outside. Dust from the horsemen rose like a cloud in the dip of the road. They would be at the barn in no time. "Go upstairs," she told Laura. "Stay there." She left no space for argument in her voice. Laura laid the scissors on the table, hurried up the stairs, and went to the window.

There were two of them on horseback. One was tall, sitting straight in his saddle, dark haired, with a wisp of a goatee on his chin. He wore a silk-banded hat upon his head. The other was like his shadow: dark, too, hunched over, following a little ways behind. They stopped, swung down. Uncle Jesse, who had suddenly appeared beneath the oak, took the horses' reins and tied them to the tree. Gesturing, they talked for a minute or two, then turned toward the house. Uncle Jesse led the way.

Laura stepped back from the window but left the curtain parted so that she could watch the men approaching the house. *Who could they be?* she wondered. Not neighbors, she was sure. As she peered through the window, she hoped for a clue, but soon the branches of the crape myrtle blocked her view.

The men were on the porch now, stomping feet, brushing clothes. Laura could hear the rattle of the windlass on the well as Uncle Jesse drew up a bucket of fresh water. The tin dipper made a clinking sound on the rim. "Thank 'ee," came a voice, scratchy, as if it had shouted too many times. The other man spoke with a smoother sound, low, so that Laura couldn't hear his words. The door opened, the men entered. Hurrying, holding her skirts so that they would not swish, Laura tiptoed across the floor to her door and cracked it so that she could see. The two men stood just below, their backs to her. Uncle Jesse introduced Aunt Charity, who waited with a pleasant smile. "Mr. Higgins," Uncle Jesse said, gesturing toward the taller man, who took off his hat and accepted Aunt Charity's hand. "Mr. Cox." He pointed to the other one.

"Thou are welcome," Aunt Charity said. "Can we get thee some refreshment?"

Mr. Higgins took a step back. Laura could see his cheeks, ruddy from his ride, his dark hair spilling over his forehead now that his hat was removed. "Thank you, ma'am. We ate on the road. We still have a long journey before us." The other man frowned, a look that said his stomach gnawed.

Aunt Charity, fluttering like a bird, began to gather up the flower-sprigged dress she and Laura had been working on. "Goodness, where are my manners?" she said. "Let me get this up so that thou will have a place to sit." She picked up the dress and her workbasket and put them on a bench at the far end of the kitchen.

Mr. Higgins reached out as if to stop her. "We don't have time to sit, either. We must be on our way. Just a few questions, that is all. Please, you sit," he said, and bowed. Aunt Charity returned, sat down, folded her hands. Uncle Jesse stood behind her, his hand on her shoulder.

"We are looking for slaves," Mr. Higgins said. Mr. Cox, standing a little apart, nodded his head. "Two slaves, as a matter of fact, who ran away recently from neighboring plantations down near Rutherfordton. Our informants, other slaves, tell us they are headed this way, or may have already passed." He stopped just a moment, his voice lingering in the air, but then went on when Aunt Charity and Uncle Jesse remained silent.

"Together or apart, we will find them, no matter who might help them in their escape."

He waited again. Aunt Charity shifted in her chair so that her skirts rustled, but she did not speak. Uncle Jesse's broad hand remained on her shoulder like a protecting shield. "A nigger girl," Mr. Higgins said finally, with a note of weariness not apparent before in his voice. "Name of Rosetta. Young, not more than sixteen or seventeen, light skin, not a mark on her, her master says. Good worker if she has the mind to do it." He put his foot up on one of the chairs, bent closer as he talked. Laura could almost feel Aunt Charity's frown. She would wash the seat when the two men left.

"The other one's called Samson. Big buck, strong, reddish skin—he's got some Indian blood. Maybe that's why he's been so unruly, always in trouble. He's got some stripes on his back to prove it. They fancy themselves married, this Samson and Rosetta. If they haven't already met up with each other, it's certainly their aim. Catch one and we'll probably catch the other. You seen them?"

The question came quickly, thrown sharply like a pebble skimmed across water. Mr. Higgins took his foot down from the chair and waited. Finally Uncle Jesse said, "No, sir. We heard the dogs a night or so ago, but nothing else. We've had no visitors except for thee. Isn't that right?" he asked Aunt Charity.

"Yes," she said quietly. Laura knew that she would ask the Lord's forgiveness in her prayers that night for lying. "No one has passed, not even a neighbor. It does get lonely at times."

Mr. Higgins smiled back at her, but his voice was less friendly than before. "Keep an eye out. You never know what you might see. Here," he said, going over to Mr. Cox. "Give them a handbill." He pointed to Mr. Cox's pocket.

Mr. Cox reached into his coat—homespun, Laura saw, ragged at the hem and none too clean. He pulled out two sheets of paper, but Laura could not see what was printed on them. "Pictures," he said. "Descriptions. There is a reward if you help find them."

Aunt Charity stood and took the papers. They would probably go into the fire as soon as the two men left. "Thank thee," she said politely, and turned away.

"We must be going," Mr. Higgins said as he put his tall hat back on. "Thank you for your time."

Bowing again, he backed away, shook hands with Uncle Jesse, and nodded to Mr. Cox. He was nearly to the door when he turned and said to Aunt Charity, "That dress. Who is it for?" He pointed to the bench in the kitchen. "It's not what I would expect a good Quaker lady to wear for meeting day. Just a little too bright." Laura could hear the smile in his voice, but she knew a trap lay in his words.

"Oh," Aunt Charity said brightly. "It belongs to my niece. I plumb forgot it was there."

"Does she live here?" His voice no longer smiled.

"No, bless her heart. We wish she did. No, she's come for a visit, my sister's child. Visits us every summer."

"Why is she not here?"

"Feeling poorly," Aunt Charity said, raising her voice a little. "That hot trip in the sun would do anybody in. She's been in bed resting practically ever since she arrived. I was just doing a little mending for her."

"I would like to see her."

Aunt Charity did not answer him at first. Then she said, "I am not sure that would be proper. She is in her room."

"I won't disturb her. It is my bounden duty to check. Shall we go upstairs?"

Laura spun away from the door, ran on tiptoes to her bed, and jumped beneath the covers, trying to press her petticoats beneath her so that the bedclothes would lie smooth. She pulled the sheet past her nose. It was too late, she realized, to remove her shoes.

"Laura?" Aunt Charity's voice came up the stairs. Footsteps followed.

"Yessum?" She tried to make her voice sound weak.

The door creaked open. Through half-closed eyes she could see Aunt Charity's worried face in the doorway. Mr. Higgins stood behind her, his eyes sweeping around the room. "My name is Higgins," he said, removing his hat again. "I am sorry to disturb you, but I had to search. Please do excuse us for being so forward."

With the sheet still covering her face, Laura said faintly, "Oh, that's all right, sir," and sighed.

"Poor thing," Aunt Charity said. "I'll have to bring thee some tea."

Mr. Higgins gave one last look around the room but said no more, and, bowing, backed out the door, hat still in his hands. Laura did not stir until she heard the front door slam. Then, quietly, she turned back the covers, sat up, and let her petticoats flare around her. She walked quickly to the window and peeked out between the curtains. Below, Aunt Charity stood at the edge of the steps, not moving, while Uncle Jesse walked Mr. Higgins and Mr. Cox toward the barn.

Uncle Jesse ambled back to the house. Ninevah, content until then to stay by Aunt Charity's feet, bounded out to meet him, barking just once at the departing figures on the road. Uncle Jesse bent down and ruffled his mane and then came to stand beside Aunt Charity. "Slave-catching scum," he said, putting his arm around her.

Aunt Charity leaned her head back against his shoulder. "Yes," she said. "Yes. But we should pray for them just the same."

Laura turned and headed for the door, then stopped in the middle of the floor. There, in plain view, lay Rosetta's rags in a little heap. Laura had not gathered them up when Rosetta had changed into Laura's dress two nights before. Surely Mr. Higgins would have seen them. How could he not? And what would he think? That Laura had arrived in such vestments? No. He would have his suspicions, might this very moment be waiting down the road to see who might pass his way with a slave somehow hidden.

Laura trembled. For the first time fear pushed excitement from her heart. But she could not tell anyone. Not Uncle Jesse, not Aunt Charity. They would never let her and Rosetta go if they thought they were in immediate danger. And certainly not Rosetta. She had already experienced enough fearfulness. No, this would have to be her secret. She would have to be constantly on guard. Even if Mr. Higgins wasn't suspicious, there would be others lying in wait, ready to betray them for a few dollars. She straightened her dress, tried to quiet her thudding heart, and turned again to the door leading to the stairs.

Uncle Jesse brought Rosetta up to the house again that night. After her supper, she joined Aunt Charity and Laura in Laura's bedroom. The quilt was again tacked over the window and the candles were lit. The dresses that Laura and Aunt Charity had altered lay spread out on the bed.

"They're so pretty," Rosetta said, smoothing them with her palm.

"Try them on," Aunt Charity said. "Thou should have enough room in them now."

Turning away, Rosetta removed the dress she had been wearing and raised her hands, and Aunt Charity slipped the ruffled dress over her head. Then she stood back, head to one side, inspecting. "Now that's a good fit if I do say so myself," she said. "Looks like that dress was made for thee. No one would ever suspect different."

Laura went over to one of her trunks, opened it, and then came back with the bonnet that matched the dress. "Here," she said. "Put this on. We'll do up your hair tomorrow, but let's see what it looks like for now."

Rosetta took the bonnet gingerly, as if she were afraid her touch might somehow damage it. Then, very slowly, she placed it on her head. Impatient, Laura quickly tied the ribbons beneath her chin, then stood back to look at her. "Doesn't she look pretty, Aunt Charity?" she said, taking Rosetta's hands and dancing her around the room. "All she needs is a pair of gloves and a parasol, and she'll fool just about anybody."

"Not quite," Aunt Charity said.

Laura stopped spinning around and Rosetta bumped into her. "What?" she said. "What do you mean?"

"Look." Aunt Charity pointed to the floor. Beneath the hem of the dress, Rosetta's bare toes stuck out. "She has no shoes. What in the world is she going to put on her feet?"

Hurrying over to the trunk again, Laura reached inside and pulled out a pair of slippers. "Here," she said, "try these." She held them out to Rosetta.

Rosetta took the shoes, sat down on the edge of the bed, and tried to push her toes inside. But they would not go. "My feet's too big," she said, her eyes glistening with tears. "I never wore no shoes before."

Raising her skirts, Aunt Charity looked down at her own shoes. Dark and heavy, they were an old woman's shoes. They would look as strange as bare toes beneath Rosetta's petticoats. "These would fit," she said, "but they would stick out like a sore thumb. Lord," she prayed, "what shall we do?"

Hardly were the words out of her mouth than she let go her skirts, snapped her fingers, and bent down for one of the candles sitting on the floor. "Come with me," she said. "I think the Lord has provided an answer."

Laura and Rosetta followed her out of the room, but instead of going down the stairs to the kitchen, Aunt Charity headed for a small door in the far wall. Laura had been through it only once before—to the attic, a dusty space hardly big enough to stand up in. Why was Aunt Charity taking them there? "Don't bump your heads," she told them as she turned the wooden block that held the door. She ducked and went inside.

The room was smaller than Laura remembered, with only one small window to provide light in the daytime. Now, the candle flame wavered, casting shadows in the corners of the room. Carefully, Aunt Charity set the candle on the floor, knelt before a horsehide trunk, and opened the lid. She leaned forward to look inside.

"It won't seem like much to thee," Aunt Charity said. "Memories, that's mostly what's here." She reached inside the trunk and pulled out a bouquet of blackened roses tied with a faded ribbon. She held it up, and petals fell. "From my very first grown-up dance," she said. "I had on a new dress that left my shoulders bare and wore my hair swept up with roses. Papa gave me pearls." She sighed, put down the flowers, and reached farther inside the trunk. "But I gave up all that for thine uncle Jesse and tucked these things away."

"Why?" Laura asked.

"Because I love him." She shrugged her shoulders. "I couldn't ask him to change his ways, his beliefs, and when I started to go to meeting and listened to the others, I understood. No outward show is needed. We do not need images of the Lord nor fine buildings to worship Him in. The light of God is truly inside us all."

Laura did not answer but watched while Aunt Charity pulled out more of her old treasures: a fan of ivory, a shawl of rose-colored silk. Finally, near the bottom, she found what she was looking for.

Shoes: cream-colored, made of soft leather, out of style, but no one would notice beneath Rosetta's petticoats. "Here," she said. "See if these fit thy feet." She handed the shoes to Rosetta. "I shan't be needing them anymore. My old boots'll do for going to meeting till they lay me out with my feet turned up."

She began to put her other belongings back into the trunk—the fan, the shawl—then closed the lid and stood up stiffly. "Come," she said. "We have got to get thee to bed."

They filed out of the attic. Aunt Charity closed the door behind them and they went back to Laura's room. Putting down the candle, she said to Rosetta, "Sit thee down and put on thy shoes. We'll give thee a pair of stockings tomorrow after thy bath."

Rosetta smiled, sat on the edge of Laura's bed, pulled up her skirt, and leaned over, carefully setting the shoes on the floor. "They sure are pretty," she said. "Lord, wouldn't my mama be proud to see me in such fine clothes."

Gingerly she took one of the shoes and undid the ties. Laura watched, holding her breath, while Rosetta slipped the soft leather over her bare toes. She pushed, and with no trouble at all her foot slid inside. "They fit!" Laura said so loudly that Aunt Charity gave her a fearful look. Quieter, she added, "They're just perfect. Put on the other one," she said to Rosetta. "We have to teach you to walk properly."

Rosetta put on the other shoe and laced them up. Laura took both her hands, then pulled her to a standing position and led her across the room as if she had been a child learning to walk. "Lord, I'll fall," Rosetta wailed, trying to keep her balance, but Laura would not let her go. Aunt Charity stood looking at the two of them struggling across the floor until, finally, she laughed and said, "Stop now, Laura. Thou will wear the poor girl out. She can do it by herself. Let her go."

Reluctantly Laura dropped Rosetta's hand and stepped back. Rosetta wavered a moment but then took one step, and another, and another. Aunt Charity said, "I told thee she could do it. With a little more practice, she'll be walking with no trouble a-tall. One more time around the room, and then the two of thee must get to bed. Chin up, Rosetta. Don't look at thy feet. Smile." She waved her arm, and Rosetta began to walk slowly around the room, her face glowing in the candlelight.

"That's enough," Aunt Charity finally said. "Take off thy shoes and dress. I'll go tell Jesse thou will soon be ready to go back to the meat house."

Laura's heart dropped. Whirling around the brightly lit room with Rosetta in Aunt Charity's old-fashioned dancing shoes, she had forgotten completely the reason they were there. For that little while it had seemed all a game again to her, hardly different from a musical evening back home, with neighbors visiting and singing and dancing. Now she remembered that dark hole in the ground where Rosetta must go once again, the scent of raw meat drifting down upon her head, and her happiness was gone. Walking over to where Rosetta sat unlacing the shoes, she reached out tentatively, touched her on the shoulder, and said, "It will be all over soon. We will get you away. You'll see."

Rosetta looked up. "Yes," she said, then went back to her shoes.

Laura began to put out the candles. Just before she pinched out the last flame, Rosetta, shadowed now as she pulled off her dress, said in a quiet voice, "Did somebody come here today? I thought I heard horses while I was down in that place. The dog, he was barking like I ain't heard before."

"No," Laura said without thinking. "No," telling a lie. She did not want to ruin Rosetta's few moments of joy by telling her about their visitors earlier in the day, of Mr. Higgins's inspection of her room and the incriminating pile of clothes he might have seen there. "No," she said one last time, and started toward the door. She, too, would have to ask the Lord's forgiveness when she said her prayers.

Chapter Nine

Leaving Home

Laura was sound asleep when Aunt Charity called up the stairs, "It's time. Thou must get up. Hurry now." The room was dark, dawn still far away and stars shining outside her window. She could hear Aunt Charity setting metal cups and saucers on the kitchen table for breakfast. Then she remembered. This was the day they would begin their journey, she and Rosetta, on the road alone, with only Ebenezer to accompany them, the threat of Mr. Higgins, or someone like him, lurking behind every tree.

She went to the washstand and splashed water on her face, then began to dress. It would be hot. Her room still held the heat from the day before, and what little air came through the window lay heavy and damp on the back of her neck. Still, she stepped into the layers of petticoats and put on her dress, fastening it at the neck with a cameo brooch her papa had given her.

When she went downstairs, it was still dark. Aunt Charity burned no candles, working by firelight and the knowledge of her fingertips to find the items she needed. "Hurry, eat," she said. "Jesse will be here soon with Rosetta, and I will need thy help for her bath." She pointed to the far corner of the room where she had tacked up a blanket. "The girl must wash. She cannot go in public smelling like salt meat. We must fill the tub with water."

Not at all hungry, Laura forced down the porridge Aunt Charity had made, ate a few bites of bacon, and drank the cup of tea set by her plate. Just as she was finishing, she heard the familiar sound of Ninevah sliding beneath the porch and Uncle Jesse's heavy boots on the stairs. Rosetta's bare feet were quiet as whispers.

"Good morning to thee," Aunt Charity said to Rosetta.

"Morning, ma'am. Morning, miss." Rosetta stood in the middle of the floor until Aunt Charity told her to sit down at the table and eat. She ate quickly and did not refuse seconds when Aunt Charity offered her more.

"Now thou must have a bath," Aunt Charity said. "Go behind that curtain and take off thy clothes and sit in the tub. Laura, you take those kettles from the fire and pour them in. Be careful now. Thou does not want to scald the girl."

They worked steadily. Uncle Jesse drew the water, Aunt Charity filled the kettles and hung them over the fire, Laura carried them back and forth to the tub behind the curtain and poured them over Rosetta's shoulders and hair. Hunched down, Rosetta sat with her eyes closed and a smile on her face, obviously enjoying the warm trickle down her back.

But her pleasure could not last. "Leave her be, Laura," Aunt Charity soon said. "She can dry herself. Rosetta, put on fresh underwear and get into Laura's old dress again. Don't waste time, now. It will soon be light."

Setting the empty kettle on the hearth by the fire, Laura turned and looked through the open doorway. Just barely she could see Uncle Jesse's shadow as he walked toward the barn with one of her trunks in his arms, ready to put on the wagon. Ebenezer would be waiting for him there, silent, beneath the oak tree.

Rosetta was finished now. Even in the low light they could see her skin glowing from the bath. "Sit thyself down," Aunt Charity told her, "and I will do up thy hair."

Aunt Charity took several large tortoiseshell hairpins from her pocket and began to comb Rosetta's hair. "It's a shame," she said, "to hide this pretty hair, but the less folks see, the better." She opened a hairpin with her teeth and clipped a curl, working quickly, expertly, while Laura watched.

She was amazed at the change in Rosetta. From a slave girl she was turning into a young lady right before her eyes. Surely no one who had known her before would recognize her now. Laura smiled in the darkness. They would do it, fool everyone, get away. She almost hugged herself in glee.

"Better hasten thyself," Uncle Jesse said, entering the house. "Dawn will be here soon. We cannot delay." He disappeared up the stairs to Laura's room, then returned almost at once with the other trunk.

Aunt Charity gave Rosetta's head one last pat. "There," she said. "Thy hair is finished. Go with Jesse to the barn. Laura, I want thee here a moment longer. Stay." She made shooing motions with her hands, the same way she did when she went to feed the chickens, and Jesse and Rosetta went out the door to the porch.

But Rosetta paused at the top of the steps, turned, and came back to stand in front of Aunt Charity. "I want to thank you, ma'am," she said, "for all you've done. I won't forget. I'll thank the Lord for you and the others as long as I have breath. And don't you fret none about Miss Laura. She'll be safe. We're in the Lord's hands."

She was about to turn again, but Aunt Charity took her by both arms. "Bless thee," she said. "Bless thy child." Even in the darkness Laura could see the glint of tears in Aunt Charity's eyes. "Yes, the Lord will keep thee. We, too, will pray." Then she pushed Rosetta away. "Now go, before Jesse fusses at me more. Laura, come inside."

Laura followed Aunt Charity back into the kitchen, waited while she went to the cupboard, opened it, reached up and took a horn cup from the back of the shelf. Laura heard coins rattling inside. "Here," Aunt Charity said, "take this. I was saving it for a rainy day. No chance of rain *today*, not with this heat, but it may come in handy up ahead." Quickly, she tied up the money in a small cloth.

"I've got some money," Laura said. "Papa gave me plenty for the trip, and I haven't spent a cent. I don't want to take your money, Aunt Charity."

"Hush now. Take it. It'll do a sight more good going with thee than staying on that shelf. We won't starve. Go get thy satchel and bonnet."

Laura went upstairs to her room. With her possessions gone, it seemed like a stranger's room, empty, unfamiliar. The bonnet hanging on a chair did not seem her own. For the first time she thought, *This is what it will be like for Rosetta and me, just the two of us alone with no one to help, pursued by Mr. Higgins.* But she would not be afraid. Of course it was her bonnet. Of course it was her bed. She had made it herself just a little while ago. It was a trick of the dawning light. Hastily, she picked up the bonnet, put it on her head, tied it beneath her chin, and grabbed her satchel. Now she was ready.

"Here," Aunt Charity said when Laura came back downstairs. She held out the money and dropped it into Laura's satchel. "Keep it safe." She paused a minute, then pulled Laura close. "Oh, my dear child," she said. "I hope this is the right thing to do. I would never forgive myself if anything were to happen to thee." She did not let go, and Laura could feel her heart beating next to her own.

She squeezed Aunt Charity, strange for her to be the one providing reassurance. "Of course it's right," she said. "We'll be just fine." Gently she pulled Aunt Charity's hands from her shoulders, held them in her own for a moment, then dropped them. Aunt Charity sighed but said no more.

The wagon was loaded when they got to the barn, still dark in the shadow of the oak tree. Bags of corn and oats, ax handles Uncle Jesse had carved while the light lasted on long summer nights, feathers from Aunt Charity's hens—they were all spread out on the hay in the bed of the wagon. On his way back Ebenezer would deliver the goods to the storekeeper, who would then fill the order Uncle Jesse had written out for Ebenezer to give him.

But there would be one extra item in the wagon today—Rosetta, hidden beneath the straw piled up between the two trunks, which were tied behind the straight-backed kitchen chairs where Ebenezer and Laura would sit. A third waited for Rosetta, but when Laura first looked at the wagon, she was afraid that something had happened to Rosetta, so carefully was she hidden. Then Uncle Jesse said, almost in a whisper as he bent close to the straw, "Thou are all right, yes?" and Rosetta's muffled voice came back right away, "Yessir, just fine."

Ebenezer was already seated in the wagon, dark in his Sunday suit, waiting. "Good-bye, my dear," Aunt Charity said, giving Laura one last hug. Uncle Jesse kissed her cheek and helped her into the wagon. Just then, the rooster crowed. As if a curtain had been drawn aside, light seeped beneath the oak leaves and lit their faces. No more was said. Ebenezer made a sound that the horses acknowledged with a shake of their heads, and they moved slowly toward the road. The wagon bumped over rough stones, tilted, righted itself. Dust flew up. Laura held herself to the seat, face forward.

But then she turned, raised one hand, waved. Uncle Jesse and Aunt Charity, their figures becoming smaller in the distance, returned the gesture. They stood there, the two of them, arms upraised for as long as Laura could see them—until the wagon passed the first rise and Ebenezer snapped the reins and the horses began to trot faster.

Rosetta lay silent beneath the hay.

Chapter Ten

On the Road

Few people were on the road that early in the morning. The windows of neighboring houses stayed dark, though the roofs were tinted pale pink and orange by the morning light and trees turned purplish on the horizon. If animals stirred in outbuildings, they were quiet, and only a few birds sang.

Sitting beside Ebenezer on the wagon, Laura at first held her body rigid on the wooden chair, each rock that jolted the wheels a little blow to her back. But then, as the day lightened and Ebenezer began to hum a hymn under his breath, she felt her body relax. The moisture on her brow was cooling even if there was no wind. She swayed with the motion of the wagon and felt at peace, the purpose of their trip tucked away.

They began to pass other wagons, packed like their own with goods for trade in town. People smiled, raised their hats. Some stared. Laura, suddenly afraid they might become suspicious, wanted to take the reins and make the horses increase their pace. Ebenezer must have felt her unease. "Don't you worry none about them folks," he said, turning to her. "They be about they own bizness." He smiled and she relaxed once more.

Sitting there, Laura realized that she had never really *looked* at Ebenezer before, even though she saw him on every summer's visit—helping Uncle Jesse clear the fields, cutting wood for Aunt Charity. He had simply *been* there, as familiar as the rocker on the back porch or the dipper by the bucket on the well. She had seen his house, ramshackle, at the edge of Uncle Jesse's property, but she'd never wondered who else might live there with him.

They rode on in silence. The sun was fully up, blazing on their backs. At a fork they turned and came to a wilder place, and Laura asked Ebenezer, "Is this right?" wondering if he could read the words on the sign.

"Right for now," he said. "We got to get that girl out from underneath that hay or she going to smother to death in this heat. We gone far enough from your uncle Jesse and aunt Charity's place that ain't no neighbors going to be about, and iffen any stranger come by, I just say you ladies refreshing yourselves by the stream."

Laura heard it then, water rattling over rocks, and just the sound made her feel cooler. Trees pushed closer to the road, and their tangled boughs brought sudden shade. "Here," Ebenezer said, reining in the horses. "This be a good enough place," and they stopped.

Quickly, turning from her chair, Laura stepped into the back of the wagon. The two trunks were not locked. She raised the lid of the nearer one and lifted out the clothes Rosetta was to wear—the dress of twining flowers, the bonnet that matched, Aunt Charity's dancing shoes. How strange it seemed to be holding them there in the middle of a deserted road on a bright summer's day.

"Better hurry, miss." Ebenezer's voice was quiet but held a tone of warning.

She slammed the lid, then jumped down from the wagon. *Fool,* she told herself, *standing there daydreaming while Rosetta lies burning up beneath the hay.* "Come on out now," she called to her. "It's all right. No one's here."

She waited, holding her breath, the clothes clutched to her. High up on the wagon Ebenezer sat motionless, waiting, too. There was no movement beneath the hay. *Is she asleep?* Laura wondered. *Worn out by the bumpy ride?* Then a worse thought came. "Rosetta, Rosetta!" she called, trying to keep her voice low. Ebenezer turned sharply to her, then got down. The horses whinnied. "No," he said anxiously, then began to pull apart the hay. Laura watched, still afraid, heart pounding as his motions became more frantic. "Rosetta, Rosetta," he whispered. "Where are you, girl? Come on out. You don't have to hide no more."

At last she appeared. A bare foot at first, then the hem of Laura's torn and muddied dress, finally the curls Aunt Charity had pinned up, covered with wisps of straw. Blinking in the light, Rosetta brushed her face, then said, "I'm all right. Hot as the dickens, but still a-breathing. Give me those clothes."

"Girl, you scared us half to death," Ebenezer said. "We thought you was *dead.* Now you go get dressed. We ain't got time for any messing 'round."

She stood then, bits of straw falling from her hair like insects swarming, got down from the wagon and walked to the back where Laura stood. Laura handed her the dress, shoes, and bonnet. "I won't be long," Rosetta said, and hurried off into the woods.

Ebenezer pulled the wagon farther beneath the trees, tethered the horses near a patch of grass, and neatened the pile of straw. Laura climbed into the wagon again and sat down beside him. "You all right?" he asked her, and she nodded her head and closed her eyes for a moment of calm.

Goodness, how her life had changed. Just a few days ago she had set out for her aunt Charity and uncle Jesse's house with nothing more on her mind than the prospect of long, lazy summer days on the farm. Now, having stumbled onto the hidden room beneath the meat house, she was on the road again, but this time she was helping a slave escape, with Lord knows what lying ahead—Mr. Higgins waiting around a bend? Other slave catchers on the road? Even another slave who might betray them for a few dollars? Calmness did not come.

Ebenezer must have perceived her thoughts. "You need to be careful, Miss Laura," he said. "There be some mean peoples in this world."

Laura opened her eyes. Ebenezer sat slightly bent over, the reins lying loosely in his hands, staring at her. "What about *you*?" she said. "Don't you have to be careful, too?"

He gave a little laugh. "They don't bother me none. I be too old. Anyway, I got my papers." He pointed to his straw hat.

"What if they knew about Rosetta?"

He sat up straighter, let a little sigh escape. "That'd be mighty different," he said, eyes looking past her into the woods where Rosetta had disappeared. "Even my papers wouldn't help none then. They put me *beneath* the jailhouse."

"Why are you doing it, then? Helping Rosetta, I mean."

"Oh, well now." He looked back at Laura. "It seems like my duty. I got my freedom, I got to help others get theirs."

"But you didn't have to run away."

"No, I was one of the lucky ones. Mr. Jesse's daddy, he bought me when I was just a boy. Near broke my heart, tearing me away from my mama like that. I never saw her again, even though I tried to find her after I got grown. She'd been sold, nobody knew where.

"Now, Mr. Jesse's daddy won't no bad man, didn't ever beat me or the other slaves he owned. He liked his corn liquor, though, I'd never deny that, and he could out-cuss anybody in the county. But marriage changed all that. He met this little bitty woman name of Miz Hattie and married her after no more than a month of courting. Before you could say *jackrabbit*, the drinking and cussing stopped and he was going off to meeting with Miz Hattie, dressed up in his Sunday suit. On his deathbed, after Miz Hattie herself had passed on, he set the slaves free, and Mr. Jesse, he followed his daddy's wishes. Did more than that—gave me the house I live in and my little piece of land."

"You could have sold it, gone off up North."

Ebenezer stared off at the woods, silent for a moment. Then he began again. "Yessum, I know. The others did—went on off, I mean. But I had other reasons for staying; it won't just the land. Two babies and their mama buried down at the edge of the woods beneath a weeping willow tree. I still keep it cleared off, that spot. Brought up smooth stones from the creek to mark the graves and planted wildflowers around. It's pretty. Next time you come, I'll show you if you want."

They both jumped at the sound of a voice. "Hey there. You-all gone to sleep?" It was Rosetta, standing in deep shade beneath the trees, Laura's bonnet tied atop her curls, her dress skimming the ground around her. "Hey," she said again when they did not answer her. Then, picking up her skirts, she stepped easily in her new shoes across the stone road to the wagon.

"Lord, Rosetta," Ebenezer finally said, a smile breaking out on his face. "You do look nice."

Laura jumped down and grabbed Rosetta's hands. "It's perfect," she said, stepping back to admire her. "Nobody will ever know. Come on. Get back up on the wagon. We've still got a long way to go."

Grinning, Rosetta climbed up as daintily as any fine lady. Laura followed her, and then they were off.

The sun was full up now, hotter than before. Laura and Rosetta turned their heads away from the sun so that their bonnets shaded their faces, but even then the glare made them squeeze their eyes shut. After what seemed like hours, Ebenezer pulled the wagon off to the side of the road and said, "These horses need a rest, and I reckon we do, too. The dinner your aunt Charity packed would taste mighty good right about now, don't you think?"

"I'd almost forgot," Laura said, jumping down. She went around to the back of the wagon and Rosetta handed her the basket Aunt Charity had packed. "Come on," she said, heading for a stand of trees. "We'll eat here." And in no time at all she had set the basket down and spread the food on a cloth on a furry tuft of moss—side meat, cheese, bread, and butter still cool in its wrapper of green leaves. "Lord, I *am* hungry," she said, her mouth watering. "Help yourselves."

Careful of her skirt, Rosetta sat down on the moss beside Laura, but Ebenezer remained standing. "Fix me a plate, please, miss," he said. "Wouldn't do for folks to pass by and see me eating with two white ladies, or what they think is two white ladies." He laughed. "I just go and set over yonder beneath them trees. I be just fine."

Laura fixed the plate and Ebenezer took it, then walked away from them and sat down beneath some low-hanging branches. *Well, how silly,* Laura thought. *Here I've been riding right next to him all day long just about touching, and when it comes time to eat, he has to go off by himself. The world doesn't make a whole lot of sense sometimes.*

They ate quickly, then rested for a brief while in the green shade. Only one wagon passed, a family on the way to market with their goods packed up on the wagon bed. Two children, bouncing in back, turned and waved and their parents nodded as they went by.

"We should be getting along, too," Ebenezer said, coming to stand beside the girls once again. Dust from the wagon wheels still boiled on the road.

"I hate to go out in that hot sun again," Laura said, but she stood and, with Rosetta's help, began to pack up the basket with the leftover food.

They rode in silence through the long hot afternoon, up and down hills, through woodland shade that provided a few moments of occasional relief. The road widened; tracks crossed from other directions. They saw farms, houses clustered close together, villages with church spires rising up like hymns sung on Sunday morning. Swaying on her seat, Laura dozed.

Then, suddenly awake, she felt Rosetta stiffen beside her, heard her cry, and opened her eyes to watch in horror as Rosetta started to climb out of the wagon.

"Girl, you lost your *mind*?" Ebenezer said, reining in the horses. "You going to get yourself *kilt*!"

But she paid no attention, gathering up her skirts as she hopped down from the wagon and scurried to the side of the road. With no hesitation, she stepped into the dusty, waist-high weeds.

"Rosetta!" Laura called out. "There may be snakes!" But Rosetta kept going.

And then Laura saw why. In front of her, nailed to a tree, was a sheet of paper with a picture drawn on it—

Rosetta's Samson, sure as anything, with WANTED! printed underneath. It was a copy of one of the handbills that Mr. Higgins had given to Aunt Charity. Mr. Higgins had come this way, and not too long before. The paper was unstained, the words unblurred. What if he returned and saw the sign pulled down? Would he be suspicious?

Slowly Rosetta returned to the wagon, the handbill crumpled in her hands. When she climbed up, Laura could see tears in her eyes. Ebenezer must have seen them, too, but he paid no mind, his own eyes slit with anger. "Fool," he said. "You done broke the law taking down that sign. Right in broad daylight, too, with other folks around. We could all go to jail. Now you set down and let us get on into town without any more of your foolishness." He snapped the reins, and the wagon rattled forward.

Rosetta was silent, her fingers gently pressing out the wrinkles in the crumpled piece of paper that lay in her lap. She did not look up again until they drove into Savannah.

Chapter Eleven

Savannah

By the time they reached the edge of the city, it was well past suppertime. The sun was long gone behind the trees, the first stars pale in the sky. They had noticed the changing landscape miles before. Farms had become smaller, closer together, sometimes a cluster of cabins marking a town that had become part of the growing city. Traffic quickened. When a church spire appeared, and then another and another, Laura said, "Oh, look!" and Ebenezer and Rosetta turned to follow her pointing finger.

They moved on, clattering over cobbled streets past mansions set around squares as perfectly laid out as a gaming table. Candlelight streamed through windows and cast golden patches on the ground, and the sounds of murmuring voices and tinkling ice in glasses flowed from the wide verandas. Over all hung long garlands of Spanish moss, and grapevines twined wherever they could gain a hold.

They turned, once, twice—Ebenezer knew the way. Laura wondered how many times he had driven along these streets. He reined in the horses, driving more slowly, eyes alert to the houses on either side of the street. The houses were smaller in this part of town, two-storied, with steps leading up to high front porches. "Here we are," he said at last and stopped before an open gate. Looking up, Laura saw darkened windows.

"You're sure?" she asked, hearing the doubt in her voice.

"Oh, yessum. Miz Webber's house. She a nice lady, couldn't ask for no better." He got down, reached up to help Laura and Rosetta, then stepped through the gate and started up the stairs.

Uncle Jesse had first mentioned her name. "In Savannah thou will stay with a Mrs. Webber," he had told Laura before they left the farm. "I have sent word ahead. She will be expecting thee. She will ask no questions. But you can depend on her for a clean bed and a good breakfast, and she can guide thee to the steamship office. Don't worry about pay."

Ebenezer knocked on the door. No one answered at first and he rapped again. In a moment a soft yellow glow appeared behind lacy curtains in the bowed front window. "Who's there?" a voice called out.

"It's Ebenezer," he said, his voice almost a whisper. "And the ladies." He waited again.

The door opened. A woman peeked out, candle held high. Suddenly she laughed. "I thought you might be haints at first," she said. "Never know who's at your door in this town. Y'all come on in. You must have had a long journey. It's late. I was about to give you out." She stepped aside and they moved past her into the narrow entranceway of the house.

She was a small woman, thin as a blade of grass, hair pulled back. "I'm Alice Webber," she said, and nodded when Laura murmured their names, using *Charlotte* instead of *Rosetta,* unsure whether or not to continue their disguise.

If Mrs. Webber had any suspicions, she did not show them, and she hurried them through a hallway to the back of the house, where the kitchen table was laid with utensils, a cloth covering up the food. "It's cold," she said as she whipped off the cloth, revealing bread and side meat and a tin of molasses, "but it'll fill you up. Then I'll get you to bed."

They ate hungrily, Laura and Rosetta at the table in the circle of candlelight, Ebenezer out on the back porch at the edge of shadows. Mrs. Webber sat watching them, face aglow, asking every now and then whether she could get them anything else, finally taking out of a tin the pound cake she must have baked fresh that day. "Lordy, I'm full as a tick," Rosetta said when Mrs. Webber offered her a second piece. She clapped her hand over her mouth, no doubt remembering that she wasn't supposed to speak. Again, Mrs. Webber seemed to take no notice.

"Bring up those trunks," Mrs. Webber said to Ebenezer when he handed her his empty plate. "Put them in the front room at the head of the stairs. You-all go on up, too," she told Laura and Rosetta. "There's fresh water on the washstand, towels. Let me know if there's anything else you need. I'll call you tomorrow morning." She turned and dunked the dish in a waiting pan of water and began to scrub.

Laura went over to her and touched her shoulder. "Thank you, ma'am. You've been kind. We appreciate all you've done."

Mrs. Webber's neck reddened. "It ain't nothing," she said, stopping for a moment to stare at the plate. "Just what little I can do for the Lord. He guides us all." Then she began to wash the dish once again.

Laura and Rosetta walked to the front of the house. Ebenezer stood there in the open doorway, his hat in his hands. "I best be going on," he said. "It's a long ways home and I've got to go to the storekeeper's for your uncle Jesse."

"Won't you get some sleep?" Laura asked. "You aren't going to drive back right away, are you?"

Ebenezer laughed. "I reckon I'll get me some catnaps. Them horses practically know the way without any help from me. I just sit up on that wagon and head them in the right direction, and they go."

He started to turn. Laura took his hand. "Thank you, sir," she said. "You have a safe trip back. And tell Uncle Jesse and Aunt Charity we're doing just fine. They don't need to worry."

"Yessum," he said, and put on his hat. "I'll remember you in my prayers, both of you. And you take good care of that baby when it comes," he said to Rosetta. "It's already been through more'n most, don't need no more upset."

"Yes sir," Rosetta said in a strong voice. "I'll do that. Ain't no harm gonna come to my child."

Ebenezer turned again and went down the stairs, untied the horses, and climbed onto the wagon. No lights burned anywhere, and the night was very quiet. When he clicked his tongue, the horses began to move and the wagon slowly rattled away. He did not look back.

"You rest," Laura said the next morning as she tied on her bonnet. "I'll be back in a little while."

Rosetta smiled. She still lay upon the bed in her underclothes, feet drawn up, hair spread upon the pillow.

"You don't have to tell me twice," she said. "I still got aches and pains from that bumpy ride yestiddy. And that young-un needs to get calmed down a little bit from all that moving around, else I'll be sick." She pointed to her stomach.

Laura smiled, too, then picked up the empty tray Mrs. Webber had brought up earlier—with glasses of cool sweet milk and freshly made biscuits on it—and went downstairs. In the parlor, bright sunlight poured through the window. Mrs. Webber was busy at the kitchen counter, preparing vegetables for the noon meal. Laura set down the tray. "Thank you, ma'am," she said. "It was mighty good."

Mrs. Webber's eyes lit up. "I'm right pleased you liked it," she said. "Traveling takes a lot out of you. Miss Charlotte doing all right?" Delight faded into concern. "She need anything?"

"Oh, no. She'll be just fine. She's sleeping now. Could you show me the way to the steamship office? I have to book our passage."

"Surely," she said, drying her hands on her apron. Laura followed her through the doorway to the front hall, then outside onto the narrow porch. "Up thataway two blocks," Mrs. Webber said, pointing, "then turn right. Keep on walking through the squares till you can see the dock ahead. There'll be signs. And if you get lost, just ask anybody who looks like they've got good sense and they can tell you the way. This is a friendly town, no matter what others might say."

Laura thanked her, then went down the stairs and opened the wrought iron gate. Mrs. Webber stood on the porch watching her, till Laura turned the corner, and Mrs. Webber was out of sight.

Laura was grateful for the trees. Their wide branches, thick with moss, protected the squares from the fierce sunlight. People strolled there or sat gossiping on the benches, dipping their hands in the basins of fountains to cool themselves. Wagons rattled past and voices called out, "Peaches, crabs, fresh-baked bread, come buy!" When a band of scrawny pigs roamed past, scavenging for food, Laura jumped aside; but a man, lifting his hat, said, "Don't be afraid, miss. They won't bother you. People let them go about. They clean up the streets."

Laura walked on, fascinated by the sights of the city, and when she saw a sign painted with a pointing finger and the words GREATER SOUTH STEAMSHIP LINES, she almost passed it by. Little more than a shed, the offices stood at the end of a narrow alleyway high above the river. She could hear shouting, a whistle, the flap of gull wings. *Too bad the pigs didn't come this way,* she thought as she picked her way down the alley, stepping carefully to avoid the offal there. Her nose wrinkled from the scent. When she went inside the office, the odor was no better.

The air was thick with the smell of tobacco smoke, boot leather, food, and drink.

Worse were the eyes, men staring at her. She was the only female there, and while the men continued to speak to one another, they looked her up and down as if she were some animal they were examining to buy. But she walked past them, eyes straight ahead, and went up to the little booth where a man sat in his shirtsleeves behind iron bars. "I want to book passage," she said, hoping her voice did not tremble.

"Where to?" he said. His voice was flat, his eyes probing. Before she could answer, he said, "Alone, are you?"

Quickly she said, "Oh, no, sir, I'm with my sister. She's feeling poorly. We had a long trip. We're going to Charleston and then on to a ship."

He asked no more questions. Reaching into her satchel, Laura took out her purse and gave him the money. After he counted the coins, he stamped two tickets and passed them to her beneath the iron bars. "Four o'clock sharp she leaves," he said. "The *Mary Muldoon*. Don't be late."

"Yes sir," she said as she took the tickets and tucked them in her purse. Glad to have the task over with, she turned and hurried toward the door.

She almost fell.

There, just a few feet away, stood a dark figure, thin as a shadow. Mr. Higgins, she was almost sure of it. Had he followed her? Was he waiting to pounce on her as soon as she left the steamship office? But he hadn't seen her face when he had come into her room at Aunt Charity and Uncle Jesse's. How would he recognize her? She took a deep breath, trying to ease her trembling heart and think what to do.

"Are you all right, miss?" said one of the men who'd stood gossiping in the room. He strode up to her and took her arm.

"Oh, yes, thank you," she said, breathing a little easier. "It was just the heat." She looked toward the doorway. The dark figure was gone. "I'll be all right," she said as she pulled away. "Thank you." And she hurried out into the alley.

The streets were busier now. Away from the shaded squares, the sun blazed down, and a stench of rot filled the air. Children chased the roaming pigs and set them squealing, and harsh voices burst from taverndoors. Laura hurried along, anxious to get back to Rosetta and away from prying eyes.

At first, walking with her head down to shield her eyes from the glare, she did not see the little group approaching. Then she realized that a sudden quiet had descended upon the streets. The vendors stopped their calling and the children hushed their teasing. Laura looked up, half afraid.

There, coming down the street, was a band of slaves, ten or twelve of them, men and women, bare feet slipping on the cobblestones. The men were chained by the wrist to an iron bar between them, while the women, carrying babies, moved freely. Older children walked along beside.

Laura stopped. The group slowly passed her. She smelled them and heard their sighs. Her chest became tight, and she could hardly breathe. She had never viewed such a scene of sorrow. Or had she only looked the other way? The slaves who worked her papa's fields must have trudged down such streets, torn from their families and their homes. Rosetta, too, might have come this way. If she were caught, she would be sent back to her old master to be punished or, worse still, sold, her child taken away, with no hope of finding Samson ever again.

She had to get back to her, to Rosetta. If she still had any thoughts that this was just play, they were purged by the sight she had just seen. Bending, she tried to catch her breath, and for a moment the world turned dark. She stumbled into one of the squares and sat in the shade, waiting for her heavy breathing to subside.

Finally her heart quieted. She wiped away her tears and hurried back to the house, where Rosetta lay waiting for her return.

Chapter Twelve

On the *Mary Muldoon*

"They should let us board soon. We're supposed to leave at four o'clock. It must be close to that now."

Laura looked up at the sky where the sun still burned. She and Rosetta sat on their trunks, deposited there by the driver Mrs. Webber had provided for them. On the way, Rosetta, refreshed by sleep and a good meal, had looked eagerly out of the carriage at the sights of the city. "Lord, I've never seen such goings-on," she had said, and leaned farther out the window.

Laura pulled her back. "Don't go revealing too much of yourself," she had warned. "You never know who might be watching."

Others waited with them on the dock, mostly men, laughing, feet propped up on their satchels and clay pipes clutched in their hands. Dockworkers scurried back and forth, loading boxes onto the ship, and a peddler came by offering fruit. Laura bought peaches and put them in her satchel.

Finally the captain appeared on the deck of the ship, a tall man who wore no hat but whose bushy eyebrows shaded his eyes. "Welcome!" he called out over the noise of the dock. A whistle blew. "The *Mary Muldoon* is ready for you, ladies and gentlemen. Come aboard."

Leaving their trunks to be put on the ship, Laura gave Rosetta her hand and they crossed the rough boards of the dock to the gangplank. *Mary Muldoon,* she read on the side of the ship. Above the name was the portrait of a woman with a smiling face and long hair that hung down like tendrils from a vine. *Whoever she is or was,* Laura thought, *I hope she protects us now.* They climbed aboard.

The enormity of the ship surprised her. Ahead, the boiler bulged with steam, making a hissing sound, and black smokestacks reared up against the sky. Cinders fell bright red around them. High, high above, a flag flapped in the breeze, and startled gulls went squalling across the river. An enormous wheel stood ready to turn at the captain's command.

"Careful, ladies," the captain said as they stepped down. He offered Laura his hand and she took it with one hand, still holding on to the satchel and Rosetta with the other. "The ladies' quarters are that way." He pointed toward a wide flight of stairs. "You-all go on up there and find a place to rest." With a little bow, he turned to greet the others as they came aboard.

Laura and Rosetta climbed up the stairs and walked along the upper deck toward a pair of mahogany doors. Beside them huge piles of logs were stacked, ready to stoke the fire beneath the boiler, each log perfectly cut like a newly risen loaf of bread set out for baking. Ropes curled snakelike on the deck.

They had almost reached the doors when they heard a commotion on the dock. "Wait! Wait!" a voice called out, and a stream of little cries followed. Stopping, almost afraid to look for fear that someone might be chasing after them, Laura turned and peered over the railing. There she saw a small band of girls, probably her own age, their faces hidden by bonnet brims but their distress plain to hear from their cries. Leading them was a woman of ample size whose feathered bonnet bobbed up and down as she ran with little steps toward the gang-plank. Even from that distance Laura could see the woman's bright red hair was not the color the Lord had given her, shocking to see.

When the group had reached the gangplank, sailors lifting the ramp dropped it with a bang that made the deck tremble, then stepped aside at the captain's command. "Oh, oh!" the woman said, waving a handkerchief like a flag as she took the captain's waiting arm. "Come along, girls," she recovered enough to say, and they quickly followed her on board like chicks after a mother hen. Laura laughed—Rosetta, too—and then they turned away. A great blast blew from the smokestacks, and with a shudder the wheel began to turn. The *Mary Muldoon* headed out to sea.

Quickly they reached the middle of the river. The dock lay behind them now; low mudflats steamed in the sun. The ship turned and headed downriver. The water churned up by the wheels was deep brown and raised a heavy, unpleasant odor, like something closed off in darkness. Laura shuddered. "Come on," she said to Rosetta. "Let's find a place to sit down."

They opened the heavy mahogany doors and went inside. After the brightness of the sun, the cabin seemed very dark, and they stood a moment waiting for their eyes to adjust. The room was not large, an open space with curtained cubicles, no real privacy. "We won't be able to talk a-tall," Laura whispered to Rosetta. "Not unless we want everybody in the world to hear us." She released Rosetta's hand, circled the room, then pointed to a corner cubicle. "Let's take that one," she said. "It's as good as any other."

Their trunks had already been set near the door of the room, and Laura dragged them over. Rosetta sat down on a narrow bench behind the half-closed curtains. Others began to come in then—women encumbered by boxes and bags, seeking out their own trunks. They nodded at Laura and Rosetta, like them looking for a more private place, then settled down with their possessions surrounding them. They pulled off bonnets, fanned their faces, brushed up stray strands of hair. Some sighed, perhaps just parted from a loved one on shore.

"My goodness! Is there no more space? I should complain to the captain about this." The voice rang out as loud as the steamship's whistle, and all eyes turned toward the doorway, where a heavy figure stood. It was the woman with her brood of girls who had almost missed the boat. "Travel is such a trial." Addressing the girls who were coming through the doorway behind her, she said, "I hope you appreciate all the efforts I have taken for your sakes."

Most of the girls ignored her, but one said, "Aw, Miss Eva, it's not so bad," and went hurrying off to claim a spot. The woman shook her head, picked up her satchel, and walked over to the corner where Laura and Rosetta sat. "Anyone here?" she asked, pointing to the cubicle beside them. Before Laura could answer, the woman dumped down her bag and sat on the bench there. "My goodness, are you two traveling alone?" she asked almost at once. "What is this world coming to? I'm afraid to let my dears out of my sight." She leaned over and whispered, "Men, you see. You cannot trust them. Be on your guard."

"We haven't had any trouble, have we, Charlotte?" Laura said. Rosetta shook her head. "My sister's sick," Laura added, "has to go up North to a special doctor. Since it's harvest time, nobody could be spared from home to come with us."

"Oh, you poor thing!" the woman said. Her face crinkled with concern. "What's wrong?"

"Her lungs," Laura answered. Rosetta ducked her head, though the woman tried to peer beneath the brim to glimpse her face. "She can hardly say a word." Rosetta gave a little cough.

"A poultice, that's what she needs. For her chest." The woman nodded to confirm her words. "Does a world of good for that kind of ailment. Roots, nature's remedies—they're the best." She looked thoughtfully at her satchel, then frowned. "Unfortunately, I have little with me of that sort of thing. Only a purge in case one of the girls has stomach trouble." She thought a moment. "I wonder if that would help."

Laura shuddered. She had seen the effects of purging back home, a person doubled over and moaning in pain. What would happen to the baby if Rosetta took some remedy like that? "Oh, thank you, ma'am," she said hastily, "but the doctor said she wasn't to have anything a-tall except food and rest."

The woman shrugged. "Oh, well, I suppose he knows best," she said, but she did not sound convinced. "I don't know that she will get much rest on this boat. Look at these accommodations." She waved her hand vaguely toward the girls who were giggling across the room. "Too public, too many people roaming around. I have to keep a careful eye out to be sure nothing happens."

"Where are you ladies going?" Laura asked to change the subject.

The woman pulled back, eyes wide with surprise. "Didn't I introduce myself? Lord, where are my manners? Miss Eva Spurgeon, director of the Medford Ladies' Academy. I'm taking my girls off to Charleston for an educational experience." She held out her hand.

Laura pressed it lightly, then Rosetta followed suit. Miss Spurgeon smiled, pride, even love, in her eyes as she looked at the others across the room. Laura followed her glance, for the first time fully aware that the girls were being chaperoned by Miss Spurgeon. They were dressed in their Sunday best, bonnets beribboned, skirts ruffled, stylish as a page from Godey's *Lady's Book.* Looking down at her own wrinkled dress, Laura felt dowdy.

"What kind of educational experience?" Laura asked.

Miss Spurgeon was surprised again. "You haven't heard?" she said. Reaching up, she pulled off her bonnet and set it on the seat beside her, then pushed at the unnatural curls that popped out around her head. "A chance of a lifetime. My girls have been looking forward to it for *weeks.* Smithfield's World-Famous Traveling Exhibition—that's what we're going to see. Part history, part science, wonders of the world you're not likely to come across again. It's a shame you'll miss it." For a moment her eyes glowed in anticipation, but then she reached over and patted Laura's head. "But I understand," she said. "You must see to your sister's health. Nothing else is more important."

She stood then, shook out her rustling skirts, and pointed to the girls. "I must see how they are doing. Leave them alone for a minute and they'll be in a peck of trouble. Now you rest here," she said to Laura and Rosetta. "If you need anything, you just ask. I reckon they'll be calling us soon for supper. Lord knows what they'll feed us."

But the food was good. Fried fish caught that day, rice spiced and cooked with onions in a way that Laura had not tasted before, peaches sweet and dripping with juice, no more than a day off the tree. They ate in a mahogany-paneled saloon at tables covered with stiffly starched cloths whitened by the sun, from plates painted with a flowery design—ladies first, safe from the eyes of men drinking in the bar nearby.

Miss Spurgeon sat at the head of the table, her voice louder than the rattle of the paddle wheel as she talked to the other passengers. Laura sat with Miss Spurgeon's girls, who hardly ate at all, too excited about their excursion to Smithfield's World-Famous Traveling Exhibition. "They have a whale, stuffed, biggest thing you've ever seen," one said. "And all sorts of real live animals," added another. Laura listened, wishing that she and Rosetta could go along like anybody else, the purpose of their trip forgotten for a little while. But then she reminded herself, *Rosetta is in danger. We have no time for shows. Be on guard.* And she continued to eat quietly while the girls talked on.

As soon as she could get away, she carried a plate of food upstairs for Rosetta. "Here," she said, removing the napkin from the dish. "It was real good. Now you eat. You need to have something in your stomach."

Rosetta shook her head "No sirree," she said. "I'll be sick as I don't know what if I do. This boat bouncing done upset my stomach something terrible. No, I'd rather go hungry."

Laura covered the food again, then put the plate aside. Maybe Rosetta would feel like eating later.

Miss Spurgeon and her girls began to drift back into the room, the girls bending close with giggles, Miss Spurgeon's own strong voice urging them to retire—though to Laura she sounded as excited as her pupils.

Finally the girls began to quiet down. Candles were extinguished, bonnets hung on pegs high up on the wall, skirts arranged to avoid wrinkling. Outside, the moon had come up, nearly full, flooding through upper windows and setting the room aglow. Breathing became as regular as the paddle wheel's endless turning.

But Laura could not sleep. The day had been too full, the night still filled with worry. So far they had proceeded on their journey without discovery, but who knew what the next moment would hold, what dangers lay ahead? She tried to put such thoughts out of her mind by singing a song her papa had sung to her when she was just a little child, and eventually it worked. Her head began to nod; she felt herself sinking into darkness.

"Oh, Lord, I feel so sick!"

Laura sprang awake. It was Rosetta calling out. All she could think of was getting her outside before she woke the others and their secret was revealed. "Come on," she said, helping her up. Rosetta groaned, but with Laura's aid she managed to rise and cross the floor to the doors leading to the deck.

The deck was empty, the polished wood silvered by moonlight. They were in open sea now and the dark surface of the water rolled and foamed with the turning of the wheel. Standing at the railing, Laura and Rosetta were sprayed with a fine white mist, and they both took in deep reviving breaths of the moist sea air "You feel better now?" Laura asked.

"Yes," Rosetta answered, and tried to smile.

They lingered at the rail. The wind had picked up, and the cooling spray on their faces almost made them shiver. Laura was just about to say, *Maybe we should go back inside and try to get a little more rest,* when she heard two men talking on the deck beneath them.

"Thank you for the invitation to leave that smokey bar and those braggarts' stories for a moment," said one. His voice was light, friendly, only slightly mellowed by drink.

"Yes, yes, indeed," came the other voice. It had a sonorous tone, like that of a preacher on Sunday morning. "When one is on a mission, his patience is quickly worn away by such frivolity. It is nice to meet a gentleman of finer sensibilities."

Laura grasped the rail as if she might at any minute be tossed overboard. She needed to hear no more to know who stood smoking just beneath them. Those broad, flat intonations—it was Mr. Higgins's voice, surely. Though she had heard him only once—those few minutes when he was talking to Aunt Charity and Uncle Jesse in the kitchen, that brief moment when he had come to her room and peered at her beneath the coverlet—she would recognize his voice anywhere. Had he traced them to this boat? Or was it just coincidence that he was there? She would have to find out.

But first she had to get Rosetta inside. No need to tell her about the danger that threatened them from below. "Come," she whispered, and took Rosetta's hand, leading her through the doors again. "You rest. I have some business to attend to." Rosetta did not respond, and Laura hoped she would not feel sick again. She hurried back to the deck.

The voices still came from below, but they were muffled, as if the men had shifted their positions and the wind was blowing their words away. She would have to get closer. Slowly, hoping that her skirts would not swish, she walked down the deck to the stairs and descended, careful to keep in shadow, then went to stand by a pile of wood stacked on the lower deck. If she stuck her head out, she could see the glow of two pipes as the men smoked with their elbows resting on the rails. Their voices came as plainly as if she stood next to them.

"Yours has been a long trip, then," said the stranger to Mr. Higgins.

"Ah, yes," he answered. "I have been on the road for days, hardly a chance to rest my head."

"Chasing slaves?" the other man said, some doubt in his voice.

"Yes. My efforts are dedicated to that end. Others talk of saving them, freeing them, but I feel just as strongly that the owners have their rights, and I will help retain them. The slaves I chase are good workers, bought and cared for by their owners. They should repay him, not run away."

The other man did not reply. Mr. Higgins went on, sounding almost as if he were talking to himself.

"One may have escaped, or be dead, a buck named Samson. He has not been seen or heard in days, and momentarily I have given up my search for him. The other, a girl called Rosetta, has eluded me so far, but I am close to her now—I feel it—and I will capture her on this very boat."

"How do you know? Why have you not already found her?"

"The waters have been muddied. She has been helped by others. First a Quaker couple in whose abode I saw her torn and dirty clothing but did not recognize it as such. Then by a niece of those two who brought her to Savannah, I know not how. Others have seen the niece, but her face is not familiar to me for reasons I won't recount. I only know that she bought two tickets for this journey with a tale about a sick sister—surely a ruse to put me off the trail—and must now be on the boat with the slave girl hidden away, in a trunk, in the hold in a box, somewhere. I just barely made the boat myself, hindered by a group of silly girls and their chaperone, so I did not have a chance to note each passenger as they came aboard. That will be changed once we land."

"What do you mean?"

"A simple plan. I will be the first to reach the gang-plank. I will remain there while the passengers disembark. Though I have not seen the girl, I have her description, and she should be easy to spot—a girl alone with her trunk, or whatever receptacle she has the slave hidden in. Then I will make my move."

"I wish you well," said the other man, though with no great enthusiasm. "But now I must get some sleep. Dawn will come early, and I have a busy day ahead." He blew out a plume of smoke, tapped his pipe on the railing, then turned and walked toward Laura.

She prayed he would not see her in the shadows. Holding her breath, she tried to stand as still as the cord of wood beside her, though she feared that the sound of her beating heart would reveal her. He came on, did not turn, passed. She could smell his tobacco, the sweetness of drink on his breath. Mr. Higgins followed along behind him without saying more, his shadow darkening Laura's hiding place for just a moment as he, too, passed. "Good night," said the stranger. If Mr. Higgins answered him, his voice was lost in the sound of the paddle wheel, and the two men disappeared into the darkness.

Laura, unmindful of the bright moonlight revealing her, ran up the stairs to the room where Rosetta lay lost in quiet dreams.

Chapter Thirteen

Escape

Laura had no thought of sleep, and if she did, her dreams would have been nightmares: loud voices, footsteps, Mr. Higgins ready to unmask them and carry them away. "Wake up, wake up," she whispered to Rosetta. She had to tell her of the danger. Before, when Rosetta had asked about the hoofbeats she had heard through the meat house floor, Laura had dismissed her questions. But now, in the darkened room, she told her the truth, how Mr. Higgins and Mr. Cox had come riding up that afternoon with inquiries about Rosetta and Samson. How he had even come up to Laura's room where she lay beneath the covers. How it had been he who had nailed up the wanted sign for Samson.

Rosetta listened quietly, but in the end it was she who tried to allay Laura's fears. "It'll be all right," she said. "The Lord will protect us. Samson's got away—I know it as good as anything—and me and my baby are going to meet up with him one of these days soon. Ain't no Mr. Higgins going to stop us. I'll fix him good if he tries. You lie down now and go to sleep." And with that Rosetta herself lay down again on the hard bench and closed her eyes.

Still, Laura could not find rest. *I will have to ask for help,* she finally thought, exhausted. There was nothing else to do. Surely there was some kind soul on the boat she could call upon. But who?

As if in answer, a loud snore came from the next cubicle. Miss Spurgeon. Why, of course she was the one! Hadn't she shown care and concern for Rosetta? Hadn't she revealed her love for her girls by the light that glowed in her eyes? Laura would go to her. She had no other choice. She would simply have to trust.

Relieved, she rose up, glanced once at Rosetta, who was still sleeping peacefully, then stood. Through the upper windows pale pink light glowed, the stars almost gone as light from the sun approached the horizon. Walking carefully in order not to wake anyone else, Laura moved to the spot where Miss Spurgeon lay, mouth open, hair slightly disheveled. Touching her on the shoulder, Laura whispered, "Miss Spurgeon. Miss Spurgeon, I need to talk to you."

"Wha—What?" Miss Spurgeon sat bolt upright, sweeping back her hair.

Laura whispered, "I need to talk to you. Can we go outside?"

Miss Spurgeon asked no more questions but got up, looked over at the sleeping girls, then motioned for Laura to follow her. Cracking the door first to check outside, she opened it wider and held it for Laura, and the two of them went out onto the deck. Just then the sun broke the surface of the water, and for a moment the world was gilded. "How pretty," said Miss Spurgeon, leaning on the rail as if the urgency in Laura's voice indicated no more than a desire to see the sunrise.

Laura looked along the deck, half expecting to see Mr. Higgins. But there were no shadows in the golden light where he could hide, and the noise of the paddle wheel would cover her words, so she turned to Miss Spurgeon and said, "We need your help. We have nobody else. Can you?" And quite to her surprise she began to cry.

"Oh, you poor thing!" Miss Spurgeon embraced her. Laura could feel the softness of her bosom, smell her lavender perfume. The gold watch Miss Spurgeon wore on a chain around her neck pressed against Laura's cheek. There in her arms Laura felt as if she were being embraced by Aunt Charity, though the two women seemed to be as unalike as any two could be. She pulled back, wiped her eyes, and began to speak.

"I can't tell you all of it, ma'am," she said, "but we need to get away from this boat, my sister, Charlotte, and I. There's someone who's following us, may wish us harm, and we have to escape. Can you help us?" She felt tears again swelling in her eyes.

"Why, child, of course I will." She gave Laura another squeeze. "I thought something else was going on. 'Hardly say a word,' indeed—I heard you two whispering and knew that wasn't the whole tale. And you didn't fool me about another thing, either. I've watched my girls over the years too closely not to notice. That little bulge in your sister Charlotte's dress, it's not just bad posture. 'That girl is with child,' I said to myself, 'a sad story but one all too common.' "

Oh, Lord, Laura thought, *she thinks Rosetta is some unlucky girl in the family way without benefit of marriage vows. And what else? That they had run off to join the child's father and were being pursued by family agents? That Rosetta was being sent away to have the child in secret while a spurned suitor still tried to trace her? Goodness, what an imagination!* But wouldn't that be fitting for Miss Spurgeon? Here she was, taking her girls off to see the wonders of the world, and at the same time she had no hesitation making up wonders of her own. But let her think what she will. If she only helped them, she could make up any stories she liked.

"Oh, thank you, ma'am. I didn't know where else to turn. What shall we do?"

Miss Spurgeon let go of Laura's hand and checked her watch. "You will disembark with us," she said. "We will soon be landing. There'll be a bustle and no one will even notice. Carriages are arranged already and there will be room for you. Once we're away, then we'll decide what else to do." She took Laura's hand again. "Come now, we must wake the girls."

Back inside, Laura went to the corner where Rosetta still lay asleep, while Miss Spurgeon woke the girls and told them to get ready to debark. They responded with a buzz of chatter so Miss Spurgeon finally had to scold them. "Remember, please, that you are young ladies, and you are to mind your manners at all times." For a moment they quieted, but by the time they had put on their bonnets and gathered up their satchels, they were making as much noise as before.

"Charlotte, wake up, it's time." Gently Laura shook Rosetta's shoulder, speaking softly, still not used to the new name. Rosetta rose straight up with a fierce look on her face, arm raised as if to ward off a blow. "Nothing's wrong," Laura hastened to reassure her. "It's time to go." She reached up and took down their bonnets. "We're going to get off with the other girls," she said. "Miss Spurgeon is going to help us. Now put on your bonnet. The sooner we get off this boat the better."

The other passengers began to rouse then, stretching, smoothing out dresses. Above, the sun broke through smokey panes of glass, and shouting could be heard from the deck outside. Laura put on her bonnet and gloves, and when Miss Spurgeon signaled to the girls to follow her, she grabbed the strap of her trunk and began to drag it across the floor. Rosetta followed her with the other trunk.

"Boy!" Miss Spurgeon called to the first deckhand she saw. He looked at her with startled eyes but obeyed when she said, "Take these trunks. They are too heavy for these girls."

"Yes, *ma'am*," he said, and rattled away across the deck with the trunks behind him.

"Well, now, that's taken care of," Miss Spurgeon said, touching her lips with a lacy handkerchief.

They waited on the deck, an island of ruffled dresses, parcels and satchels, and bobbing feathers on stiff-brimmed hats. The sun shone down upon them, already too warm. Rosetta and Laura stood in the middle, surrounded by the other girls, who asked no questions, too excited about their own adventures to wonder about their presence. Laura looked about, trying to spot Mr. Higgins, but so far he had not appeared on deck.

A cry went up then from the crowd as land appeared on the horizon, just a tiny speck at first but growing larger every moment with the turning of the giant wheel. Gulls flew out to meet them, and as they approached the harbor they could see figures on the shore, waving in greeting. With a shudder, the boat slid to the dock. The anchor was dropped, the gangplank was lowered, and the first few passengers prepared to hurry down the rough boards to waiting arms. "Let us go," Miss Spurgeon said. "The carriages will be waiting," and the little band began to move.

It was then that Laura saw Mr. Higgins jostling to take his place by the gangplank. Though she could hardly breathe, she managed to warn Rosetta, "Keep your head down. He's there, looking. Don't let him see your face." She bent her own head, hoping that her bonnet brim would hide her.

"Who? Where?" Rosetta said loudly, her pose of silence forgotten, her head upright.

"Mr. Higgins, at the gangplank. Stay down and pray he doesn't notice us."

But it was too late. Mr. Higgins had seen them, his look as sharp as a ray of light in a dark room. He increased his pace, running now, never taking his eyes from Laura's and Rosetta's faces. *We're lost,* Laura thought. *There's nowhere else to go.*

Then it didn't matter. Mr. Higgins, in his pursuit, did not see the heavy rope curving in his path across the deck, did not feel its coil around his leg, and he tripped and fell over the railing with a yelp of surprise into the murky water.

"Man overboard! Man overboard!" someone shouted, and the captain ran down the gangplank, followed by two of the ship's hands, who jumped into the water and swam to the spot where Mr. Higgins had sunk.

But their help was not needed. Mr. Higgins's head suddenly appeared above the water, hair streaking down his face, finger pointing to where Rosetta stood pale as a ghost. "That's her, she's the one, seize her! I recognize that dress!" Looking at Rosetta, Laura saw, too, that the flower-sprigged dress Rosetta wore was the one Mr. Higgins had seen in the kitchen at Aunt Charity's. She took a step forward, ready to help Rosetta, but one word—"Stop!"—prevented her as Miss Spurgeon moved to her side. "Stay with the girls," she said, and hurried them toward the gangplank. Pulling at Rosetta's sleeve, she turned her bodily so that she was in the midst of the girls, then she bustled them all down the gangplank. They stepped inside the waiting carriages and drove away to the sound of Mr. Higgins's crying, "Stop, stop!" but to no avail, from his watery pool.

Chapter Fourteen

Smithfield's World-Famous Traveling Exhibition

They rode without speaking through the streets, past tall white houses pretty as frosted cakes set out for a party. On the seafront, finely dressed ladies and gentlemen promenaded, while children played with hoops, dashing between carriage wheels. No one seemed to notice when a band of buzzards dropped down to eat the offal from the gutters, their carrion scent a blight upon the day.

"Whew!" Miss Spurgeon said, waving her hand in front of her face. "I don't know which is worse, pigs or buzzards, but I suppose you have to have something to clean up the streets." She shifted in her seat across from Laura and Rosetta, her skirts ballooning up around her, and the two girls who sat beside her squeezed together to give her more room. "It won't be much longer," she said, then closed her eyes as if she prayed.

They turned away from the water. Dwellings became more modest and the paved road became a dusty track. Rosetta coughed, and Laura looked sharply at her, afraid she might become sick again after all the excitement on the dock. "Are you all right?" she asked. Rosetta smiled beneath her bonnet and nodded, and Laura lay back, relieved, her worries fading. They were in other hands now and would have to depend on Miss Spurgeon's help to speed them on their way, safe from Mr. Higgins. No doubt he was already making inquiries at the dock, trying to find out in what direction Miss Spurgeon and her group of girls had gone.

They stopped in front of a plain house, obviously a farmhouse once, added on to so that gables sat at odd angles to each other, giving it a lopsided look. The woman who came out to greet them, however, was as solid as a rock. Short, wide, face gleaming, she rushed out calling, "Miss Spurgeon, girls, welcome! Come on inside right this minute and wash up. You must be starved. I'll have dinner on the table in no time."

Her name was Eliza Haskell, to her friends, Mrs. *Simon* Haskell to anybody else. He—Mr. Haskell—was never around when you needed him, she told them, laughing, while they ate; and indeed he did not appear until much later when the meal was finished and everything was put away. She fixed him a plate in the kitchen, then left him alone while she gossiped with Miss Spurgeon on the porch, and he disappeared without notice.

They had known each other for years, Eliza Haskell and Eva Spurgeon—met at school long before Miss Spurgeon started her academy for young ladies, so, naturally, when she began to bring her girls to see the wondrous sights in the city, she lodged them at Eliza Haskell's boardinghouse. "It's a safe place," she assured their parents. "Respectable. You won't have to worry one minute about them." Mrs. Haskell fed them well, fresh butter beans and corn and tomatoes, with thick slices of pink ham and cakes dripping with frosting. While she and Miss Spurgeon rocked on the porch, the girls strolled about the yard or swung on the heavy rope swing hanging from the China tree in the front yard, skirts swooping out like sails behind them.

They went to bed before dark, but even then no one was ready for Miss Spurgeon's voice the next day when it came roaring down the hallway like a summer storm. "Rise and shine, rise and shine, it's time to greet the world good morning."

Laura laughed and stretched. The feather bed was damp beneath her. When she rose and went to the wash basin to wash her face, she felt a slight breeze coming through the window. The sky was bright blue, unmarked by clouds, and the sun would be full up soon, blazing. She combed her hair, put on her other good dress—the one still unwrinkled from traveling—and took down her bonnet from a peg on the door. "You rest some more," she said to Rosetta. "No need to get too friendly with the girls. It'll just make them ask questions. I'll bring you up some food."

"You won't hear any fuss from me," Rosetta said. "Ain't no bed ever felt quite so good before. And the baby must like it, too; quit that kicking for a while." Laura could hear her laughter all the way down the stairs.

The other girls drifted in, faces glowing with excitement. "You eat up, now," Mrs. Haskell said as she trundled back and forth from the kitchen with platters of food. "You'll have a lot of walking to do today and you'll need your strength." They required little encouragement and held out their plates when she offered more. Miss Spurgeon, eating daintily at a corner table, kept a watchful eye over them.

"Well, well, what have we here? My, what a lovely group of ladies. Aren't I the lucky one?"

The words startled them, and the girls dropped their forks and turned toward the doorway from which the deep voice came. A gentleman stood there, short, round-bellied, wearing a bright yellow vest and a tight brown suit, his bushy sideburns making him look like some kind of giant insect. He swept off his hat and bowed, and Mrs. Haskell, eyes bright, set down the platter of meat she was replenishing and ran over to him. "Good *morning*," she said, and looked as if she might take his hand. Instead she turned back to the girls and said, "Ladies, I have the honor of introducing the proprietor of Smithfield's World-Famous Traveling Exhibition, Colonel Gordon Smithfield himself. He, too, is a guest. It's not the first time he has honored us with his presence."

The colonel smiled and said, "Where else would I find such splendid accommodations, such delicious food, and, this time"—he winked—"such a lovely view? It is I who should be honored." Ushered in by Mrs. Haskell, he sat down at the table with Miss Spurgeon, who immediately became all fluttery, nearly knocking over her coffee cup. She held out her hand, and the colonel took it in his big paw. No one would have been a bit surprised if he had raised it to his lips.

The girls finished their breakfast, more nervous and excited than ever. Colonel Smithfield, with a large white napkin tucked into his collar, ate all the food Mrs. Haskell piled on his plate, while Miss Spurgeon broke off small bites of bread, buttered them, and put them carefully in her mouth.

Colonel Smithfield suddenly jumped up. "My goodness," he said, pulling out a large pocket watch. "Look at the time. You'd think *I* was the one going to view the sights instead of being responsible for them." He removed his napkin and then, with another bow to Mrs. Haskell and Miss Spurgeon, smiled and said to the girls, "Enjoy the exhibition, ladies. I am sure you will learn new and wondrous things here. I will watch for your coming. But now I must go." He took his hat, brushed his hands over his wild whiskers, then hurried through the door.

"Well, now," Miss Spurgeon said. "We'd better get on our way as well. The sun will be broiling hot soon. Carry a parasol. Remember your complexions. No gentleman is going to look at burned and blotched skin."

Laughing, the girls jumped up, went back upstairs for bonnets and parasols, and soon came down again, ready. Laura took up the plate of food Mrs. Haskell had fixed for Rosetta and set it on the table beside the bed. "You're sure you'll be all right here by yourself?" she said, sudden worry clouding her mind. "You'll miss the exhibition."

Rosetta laughed, pushed the sheet from her body, and sat up. "I'll be just fine," she said. "You go on and have a good time. There'll be other exhibitions come along when I get away up North. Won't hurt to miss one now." She said no more as she began to eat, and Laura, relieved, left her and went back down the stairs to join the other girls.

They set off down the road walking in twos and threes. "It's not far," Mrs. Haskell called to them as she pointed from the porch. "No more'n half a mile, and shaded this time of day. You won't even need your parasols." But Miss Spurgeon put hers up anyway, while she stepped carefully trying to avoid the dusty tracks of the roadway. The girls surged ahead, eager, unmindful of the heat and dust.

Soon, around a bend in the road, the exhibition came into view. "There it is!" A cry arose, and several of the girls picked up their skirts, ready to run. But then Miss Spurgeon's voice rang out, "Quit that bellowing! Remember that you are ladies, not a bunch of heathens," and they dropped back, faces red with embarrassment. Miss Spurgeon gave them one more warning look, and marched on toward the exhibition.

It was set up in a meadow, no doubt rented from some farmer, that gently rolled down to a stream where weeping willows grew, their pale green leaves shimmering with each breeze. Dark oaks bordered the grassy slope, and in the center, wagons had been pulled together in a rough half circle, with tents stretching out behind. Already visitors roamed among the exhibits, trodding down the grass, and a woman, probably the farmer's wife, and her daughters ran busily back and forth selling sweet cider and cakes and dippers of cool water from the well at their nearby house. Dust rose up over all.

"I'll never keep up with you girls," Miss Spurgeon said, already a little breathless as she stopped by the path that led into the field. "Go ahead, see what you will. You have money. But watch your purses. You don't know what kind of riffraff might be here today." Fanning her face with her hand, she stepped aside, and the girls rushed past her toward the exhibits.

Laura followed along, as eager as they. Traveling shows rarely reached the back country where she lived, but when posters appeared on trees advertising some sort of entertainment, however educational it might be, her mother would say, "A waste of money. Sinful, going off to see such things. God's mistakes." She would not let her go, even when her papa took Henry off to see the sights. Henry would come back, smug, and tell her what he had seen. Now *she* was the one to view wondrous things—but this visit would be her secret once she returned home.

They came first to a tent where animals were kept. They placed their pennies in the palm of the wrinkled and dirty man who stood by the canvas flap and went inside. Immediately they were assaulted by the scent, sharp as a barnyard, hanging in the overheated air. A chemical scent, too, worse than the other: a smell of decay that they could not at first identify.

But no matter about that, Laura thought, even though the odor might cling to her dress all day long. She was too excited by what she saw there: a bear in a cage, rattling the bars, his fur black as midnight; two monkeys with perfect white teeth set in a grin; a bison standing in the corner silently chewing, his ragged coat flaring out as if blown by prairie winds. Till that moment, such creatures had only been pictures in books to her, illustrations by artists who themselves might never have seen the animals. Now they stood in front of her not two feet away, living, breathing creatures who stared at her with wild eyes.

Then she looked closer and saw that the bear's dark coat was dulled, rubbed raw in spots by the chains that bound its feet. The monkeys' sad smiles held no joy, and the bison's flanks were gaunt. Worse still was what lay beyond the animals on the bed of a large wagon, a whale that must have been washed up on some foreign shore and then preserved, its leathery skin giving off a chemical odor that stung her eyes. It was lashed to the wagon, its tail trailing in the dusty weeds of the meadow, its huge body deflated.

Poor thing! Laura thought, remembering the vast ocean spaces she and Rosetta had briefly sailed upon. The whale would have roamed such waters, alive, coat glistening in the sunlight, its spout streaming into the sky. Now it lay dead and dull on the boards of a wagon far from shore, an object of wonder for all to see for the price of a few pennies. "Let's go," someone whispered, and Laura quickly followed the other girls as they filed outside through the opening of the tent.

"Whew," Laura said, and breathed deeply once they were outside, the dry, bitter scent of the trampled weeds a welcome relief from the smells inside the tent. "What else is there to see?" she asked one of the girls.

"Over there," she answered, leading the way. "The diorama. Miss Spurgeon told us to be sure to see it. It's the most educational thing of all. Come on."

Laura followed, unmindful of her skirts as she hurried toward the tent. Its banners hung limp against the sky: SEE HISTORY RIGHT BEFORE YOUR EYES. FOLLOW THE HAND OF DESTINY FROM ANCIENT TIMES TO THE PRESENT. Once inside, the girls peered down at a series of miniature scenes, each one perfect in detail, with handcarved figures set amidst houses, streams and oceans represented by mirrors reflecting bluish light, and dark forests. There were pyramids and battling ships and kings dressed in splendor, and rising up right in the middle of it all was a hand, carved but lifelike, set upon a rod that could be moved back and forth.

"The Hand of Destiny," a voice cried out, and when Laura looked up, startled, she saw that it was Colonel

Smithfield, in his bright vest and tall hat, who controlled the hand. "Welcome, ladies," he said with a smile. "Come join us on our trip through the wonders of the past."

Blushing just a little, Laura moved closer and watched while the Hand of Destiny moved from one scene to another and Colonel Gordon Smithfield, his voice bell-like, described what lay before them.

He told them of the days of ancient Egypt when heathens worshiped strange gods and crocodiles. Guided them across the Sea of Galilee where Jesus walked with his disciples. Took them along on the journeys of pilgrims across foreign lands, describing the pilgrims' torture at the hands of infidels. Sea battles and royal fields and America's own wars came into view, each one designated by the Hand of Destiny, which moved with more and more of a life of its own through the scenes. "Each must follow his own destiny," came Colonel Smithfield's sonorous voice. "No one can escape what is allotted to him. We must persevere until the end."

Standing there, Laura wondered if, indeed, this journey was part of a destiny determined by a power beyond her. Was there some sure hand guiding her that would see her through to the end? Or was it all happenstance, without rhythm or reason? Suppose she simply stood alone, like some figure perched in darkness on the side of a great abyss, responsible not only for herself but also for Rosetta? She shuddered a little, as if a shadow had passed over, and she did not hesitate when someone said, "Let's go now." She walked with the others out into the sunlight.

The girls ate after that, bought cakes and cider cool from the springhouse that sat over the stream at the lower end of the meadow. The farmer's daughters eyed them shyly, no doubt comparing their own dull dark homespun dresses to the brighter patterns of the store-bought cloth that made up the visiting girls' clothes. "Let's go sit over there," Laura said, pointing to a tree at the edge of the field, slightly embarrassed by the staring eyes. They hurried across the field to the welcoming shade and spread their skirts and ate their food there, surveying the crowd.

Then they dozed. The buzz of the crowd was lulling, and a breeze stirred the leaves every now and then. They had walked a ways that morning, and there had been no place to sit for the exhibitions. But there was still more to see, even though they might be tired, and so, after they finished their cider and the last crumbs of the sweet cakes, they jumped up after dozing, brushed their skirts, and rejoined the roving crowds.

"Look," said one of the girls, pointing to a knot of people gathered in a semicircle, "a profile cutter. I want to get mine done." She hurried over, already digging in her purse for money, and the others followed her. Laura had seen a few such profiles before, framed and hanging on a ribbon in someone's front parlor, but she had never seen the cutter at his work. Now she watched, fascinated, as the heavy black paper turned in his hands and a likeness of the woman who sat for him emerged as true as any painting or drawing could ever be. The crowd applauded when he had finished and mounted the silhouette, and the woman went away with her likeness carefully clutched to her breast.

"Who's next?" cried the cutter, and the girl who had rushed up said, "Me, me," and sat down on the little folding stool in front of him.

Laura looked at him. Young, hardly any older than her brother, he had long flowing hair that curled at the ends, a pale gold color that shone in the sun. Straight, much darker brows gave him an intense look, but when he caught Laura's gaze and smiled, his blue eyes were playful, like those of a little child. She watched his fleet fingers as he cut the paper's edge and knew that she must get her own likeness done.

He finished in a moment, and as if he were already aware of her intentions, he opened his hands in a welcoming gesture. Removing her bonnet, she hurried over and sat on the camp stool. She could feel his eyes roaming over her. First her hair, then her face, then her bosom, where her heart beat faster. The others who stood around them smiled and pointed as he worked, but their faces blurred in Laura's view, and all she saw while she listened to the snip-snip of the scissors was the cutter's bent head and the flash of his pale fingers.

Then he was done. The audience clapped, murmured. Some began to search their purses for coins to have their own likenesses done. But when he came up to Laura, still seated on the stool, and showed her her profile, he refused the money that she proffered. "No," he said in a low voice. "All I ask in return is that the sitter have a cup of cider with me." He dropped down beside her on one knee and signed his name, Tobias, on the back of the white card. Laura took it, eyes turned down, nearly speechless. "Th-Thank you," was all she could think to say.

"You *will* have that cider?" he said as he stood, hand held out to help her up.

"Oh, yes," she answered, and felt his long fingers take her hand.

He closed his box of supplies and folded the stool. When he propped a sign against them—CLOSED—others in the crowd sighed and began to put their money away. He did not speak as he and Laura walked across the well-trodden weeds of the meadow, but Laura was aware of the sun on his hair, the dry scent of his clothes. When he handed her a cup of cider, she saw his eyes close up and felt as if she looked into a bright blue sky.

"Let's sit here," he said as they approached one of the willow trees by the stream. Laura nodded, still too entranced to speak.

They sat there for what seemed a very long time, talking of small things—where Laura was from, Tobias's adventures on the road, where the exhibition would travel next—but to Laura every detail seemed momentous, and she tried to commit his words to memory, to go over later and enjoy. When the sun sank a little lower and Tobias took out his watch and said, "I must go now. It's getting late," she wanted to cry out, *No! No!* But all she said was, "Thank you for the cider," and shook his hand. He held it much longer than she ever would have supposed and then reached over and kissed her cheek. She didn't know whether she wanted to cry or shout with joy as she watched him disappear into the crowd.

Wandering, her mind still on Tobias, Laura did not at first pay attention to the man who stood by the entrance of the large tent where the afternoon show would be, holding his hand out for money. "Step this way, miss," she heard him say. "Watch your step. You wouldn't want to tear your skirt." His eyes were red and his teeth were stained, and she could smell whiskey when she passed him. Inside, most of the other girls were already seated on long benches set in rows amidst the weeds. A flap of canvas separated them from the men's section, though they could hear quite clearly the rough voices that rose up there and had to close their ears to avoid hearing the jokes being told.

Then, through an opening in the back of the tent, Colonel Smithfield pranced, more dandified than ever. He had traded his yellow plaid vest for a red-and-white-checkered one, and he wore trousers the color of fresh cream. The head of his cane flashed golden in the light. "Welcome, ladies and gentlemen," he said in a booming voice. From somewhere behind him came the roll of a drum, and he bowed low before the audience.

"You have seen the true wonders of Colonel Smithfield's World-Famous Traveling Exhibition," he said, standing tall again, a serious tone suddenly in his voice. "You have learned of foreign lands, viewed their wild creatures, examined the lessons of history. The mistakes of Mother Nature have passed before your eyes. But now"—his voice brightened—"we have something for your entertainment, live wonders of a different sort. You will be astounded . . . amazed . . . at the feats of our artists. You will catch your breath at their daring. Give them your attention, your applause; your visit to Colonel Smithfield's World-Famous Traveling Exhibition will be even more an experience to remember and treasure all your lives."

Again he bowed. The drum rolled, joined by a flute and fiddle, and a jaunty tune filled the tent. The men stomped their feet in time and dust rose up in a cloud to the top of the tent. "Oh, look!" the girl behind Laura shouted as the flaps at the back of the tent opened and in came four tall men dressed in spangled costumes, their legs encased in white tights, embarrassing to see.

"The Flying Balducci Brothers!" Colonel Smithfield called out. "Coming to you direct from their European triumphs." And while his words still hung in the heavy air, the men rushed forward to the center of the tent, twirling, balancing, throwing each other high. Other performers followed them, accompanied by the musicians' play: a juggler who kept bright balls and china plates whirling high above; a clown so short that Laura at first thought he might be a child, but then, looking closer, she saw that it was a man with a head and body just like anyone else but short little legs that made him waddle when he walked. He pranced, stumbled, fell, and looked wide-eyed at the audience, as if surprised to see them there.

Finally came the rider. With another roll of the drums, the canvas curtains parted, and there stood a man on the bare back of a horse, golden in the last light of the day. He, too, wore spangled tights, his hair flying in the wind, and it seemed to Laura that horse and rider merged into one flying figure galloping around the center of the tent. "Tobias!" she whispered as she recognized him. He was no longer the profile cutter sitting in the midst of a dusty meadow but a fine creature balanced on the back of a horse. The sight squeezed her heart with both pleasure and pain, and she hoped no one saw the tears forming in the corners of her eyes. She watched without breathing while Tobias flew around the tent on the back of the horse and finally disappeared through the flaps, accompanied by the sounds of applause and the heavy stomp of feet.

"You going to sit here all night?" one of the girls said. Laura looked up and saw the others rising around her and realized that the performance was over. She quickly wiped away the tears, stood, and checked her purse to be sure that the profile was safe inside. The sight of it made her think of Tobias again and she smiled. Then, able to breathe once more, her cheeks dried by a sudden breeze, she followed the others slowly out of the tent.

All the way back to Mrs. Haskell's boardinghouse, Laura was silent. When Miss Spurgeon said worriedly, "Are you sick, honey? Did you eat something that didn't agree with you?" she shook her head and kept on walking toward the sunset.

Chapter Fifteen

Back into Hiding

". . . and we thank Thee, Lord, for Thy wondrous works which we have seen today, for Thy mysteries upon this earth. Bless us and keep us through this night and forevermore."

Miss Spurgeon's voice, softer than usual, spread out over the girls like a coverlet as they knelt in Mrs. Haskell's front parlor for a bedtime prayer. Tired from the exhibition, they could hardly stay awake, eyelids drooping, heads swimming with the sights they had seen. As soon as Miss Spurgeon released them, they would clamber up the stairs to bed and to easy sleep, no desire to whisper further by candlelight.

Laura hardly heard the words. All the way back to the boardinghouse, as the night closed down around them and lightning bugs appeared beneath the trees, she had walked as if in a dream, the figure of Tobias on the flying horse before her eyes. Mrs. Haskell's good supper waiting for them hot on the table when they returned tempted her not at all, and she ate without tasting, fork moving mechanically from her plate to her mouth.

She had tried to tell Rosetta about him. "Oh, you should have seen the rider," she said. "He stood upon his horse in his bare feet and went galloping around in a circle so fast you could hardly see him. His hair flew out like the horse's mane, and his costume sparkled in the light. Look, he cut my profile and signed his name, Tobias. I will treasure it all my life."

"Lord, Lord. Don't tell me you done gone and fell in love with that boy," Rosetta said, laughing. "You got to watch out for that kind of traveling man. I heard about 'em back home. Get you with a baby and then leave you with your reputation gone." Rosetta laughed again, but Laura didn't answer, her face beet red from embarrassment.

". . . in Jesus' name, amen." Miss Spurgeon finished her prayer, then slowly pushed herself up from her knees, her nightcap quivering slightly atop her unruly hair. "Go on up to bed," she said to the girls, puffing. "Mrs. Haskell and I will have a quick cup of tea, then we'll be up. Go now. You'll have another busy day tomorrow."

The girls needed little urging. Murmuring good night, they went up the stairs to their rooms and quickly climbed into bed. In no time at all they were asleep, the only sounds in the house their soft breathing and the tinkle of teacups in the parlor below.

Laura slept deeply, too, and at first, when she heard the knocking on the door downstairs, she thought it was only a dream. But then she heard Rosetta whisper, "Wake up, wake up, Laura. They've found us!" She jerked awake, heart pounding, and knew it was real. *Maybe it's not us they're after,* she tried to fool herself into thinking, *just some late-arriving guest of Mrs. Haskell's trying to get in the door.* But there was something about the insistence of the knocking—it came again, louder—that told her it was Mr. Higgins at the door. She took Rosetta's hand, trying to keep her own from trembling.

There were footsteps on the stairs, then a rustling of skirts. The door of the room opened and Mrs. Haskell stood there, ghostly in the moonlight. Her easy smile had faded, and her brow was wrinkled with consternation. "Come, girls," she whispered to Laura and Rosetta. "We must hurry." And without question they got out of bed and followed her down the stairs into the darkness. At the bottom stood Miss Spurgeon, her face indistinct but her nightcap luminous in the light that came through the shutters. "It's all right," she said, but when the pounding came again on the door, they could see that her ribbons trembled.

Mrs. Haskell led them to the parlor. Just a few hours before, Laura had sat there half listening to Miss Spurgeon's bedtime prayer and dreaming of Tobias. Now she stood shaking in the middle of the floor, half expecting Mrs. Haskell to open the door and hand them over to their pursuers. Instead she bent over, grasped the edge of the carpet, and flipped it back. The outline of a trapdoor, nearly invisible, was revealed. Breathing hard, Mrs. Haskell took hold of a metal ring set in the door and pulled, and the door swung open easily. Stairs descended.

"Hurry!" she said. "We have no more time." And quite firmly she took hold of Laura's arm and guided her and Rosetta to the dark opening. In the brief moment that it took them to climb down, Laura saw the outlines of a small room of cut stone furnished with a cot, a table, and a chair. There was no light, though a candle sat unlit on the tabletop. "Don't make one peep," Mrs. Haskell warned as she slowly let down the door. It closed with a sigh. They heard her flip the carpet back over the floor above them, and then they stood in darkness deeper than the bottom of a well.

Though it seemed like hours, Laura knew that only moments had passed before footsteps shuffled overhead.

There was a grunt, a squeak, and then Miss Spurgeon's voice as clear as if she were right next to them, saying, "All right, Mrs. Haskell, I'm ready." The squeak came again, and Laura knew that Miss Spurgeon sat directly on top of the trapdoor, rocking in a rocking chair.

"Right this way, sir," came the sound of Mrs. Haskell's voice, along with heavy boot steps. "This is Miss Spurgeon, Miss Eva Spurgeon, director of the Medford Ladies' Academy." Her voice was sweet as honey. Laura wondered if she bowed.

"Evening, ladies," came a man's voice. "I'm sorry to disturb you like this, but I have important business." Laura knew that voice at once, even before the man introduced himself. Determined, under a cover of politeness, the voice had come creeping up the stairs at Aunt Charity and Uncle Jesse's house. Mr. Higgins, no doubt about it. He had traced them there.

". . . a slave girl by the name of Rosetta, light-skinned, young, aided and abetted by a Quaker family that helped her get aboard the boat here from Savannah. I almost had them until I met with an unfortunate accident and they got away."

The squeaking above them stopped. When she spoke, Miss Spurgeon sounded like some queen upon her throne, her embroidered skirts spread out around her. "What has that to do with us, sir? Why have you come banging on this lady's door in the middle of the night? I am here with my girls to see the wonders of Colonel Smithfield's exhibition. I know nothing about runaway slaves."

"But you must. They were seen getting into a carriage occupied by other girls, some of yours, no doubt. I have asked at many other households and all fingers point here. I cannot be wrong."

"Oh, but you can!" Miss Spurgeon's voice boomed out. "I keep careful watch over my girls. Their parents trust me. I know who is, or is not, in a carriage I might have hired. No, you are mistaken, sir. There is no stranger among us, just my own sweet girls on an educational outing."

The squeaking began again, faster this time. They could hear Miss Spurgeon's toes tapping the floor each time the rocker went forward. When he spoke again, Mr. Higgins, too, seemed more agitated, his polite tone gone. "I cannot accuse a lady of telling a lie," he said, "but I'm afraid *you* are mistaken. You must let me search."

It was Mrs. Haskell who spoke up this time. "Indeed, you cannot. There are young ladies here in their nightclothes. I will not have my reputation ruined by a slave catcher making strange claims. I would like you to leave, sir. Now. No doubt every guest in the house has been awakened by you. It is time for you to go."

Mr. Higgins's voice sounded like something ripped apart. "You will regret this, ma'am. I will return. There are laws, people to carry them out. I will be watching."

If he said good-bye, Laura did not hear it. The only sound that reached their stone-walled room was the echo of his boots as he strode through the parlor to the porch outside. After that, all was quiet.

They did not know how long they stood in darkness, unable to move, afraid to speak. Laura's legs ached from her visit to the exhibition that day, and she worried that Rosetta, in her condition, would soon tire. Finally, as the silence continued above, she took Rosetta's hand and whispered, "Stand still and hold my hand while I feel around for a place to sit. That cot can't be far away." And using Rosetta as a still point, she moved slowly around her, hand stretched out, until her fingertips touched the cot and she was able to grab the rough covering. "Move over here," she said to Rosetta, and gave her a little pull toward her. Rosetta sat down beside her.

She mustn't sleep. Mr. Higgins might return, bring the law, search the house. Miss Spurgeon might be moved from her rocker atop the trapdoor. But if that happened, there was no escape, no way out of what already seemed like a prison. She shook her foot, patted Rosetta's hand, hummed a little tune, yet could not keep her eyelids from drooping. When Rosetta roused her, she was sleeping soundly.

"Someone's coming!" Rosetta whispered, and then Laura heard footsteps above, the swishing sound of skirts again, finally the thump of the rug turned back, the whoosh of the trapdoor being lifted. A pale light gleamed from above and blinded them. "It's all right," a voice came. "They're gone. You don't have to be afraid." And Mrs. Haskell's kind face shone above them like a moon. Carefully, she came down the stairs and set her candle on the table next to the cot. Laura and Rosetta still sat there, and Mrs. Haskell drew up the chair and sat beside them.

"Don't be afraid," she said again, clasping Laura's and Rosetta's hands. "I don't think he'll be back tonight. He may be watching the road, but he'll stay away from the house for now. Anyway, I've got Mr. Haskell out on the porch watching in the dark, poor thing; but he doesn't really mind."

"What about Miss Spurgeon? The girls?" Laura spoke out loud, and the sound of her voice almost frightened her.

"Fast asleep." Mrs. Haskell laughed. "The way you're going to be as soon as I've talked with you for a few minutes. But I need to explain first. This"—she glanced around the hidden room still shadowed in the corners—

"this room has been used before, you must have guessed, by others trying to get away from bondage. We do what little we can, Mr. Haskell and I. No high-sounding reasons, nothing about religion—it's just that it strikes us as wrong for one person to try to own another and treat them bad. When you two arrived with Miss Spurgeon and she told me her romantic tale, I already had my suspicions, and then that awful Mr. Higgins came along and I knew we'd have to continue to hide you, the way we've done with others. Now we will have to help you escape."

Mrs. Haskell looked up at the dark square of the trapdoor in the parlor floor as if a rescuer awaited them there. But no figure appeared, and when she turned back to them, she looked worried. "I have a plan," she said. "It's dangerous, it'll be uncomfortable, but it should get you away from Mr. Higgins without his even knowing it. That would give me some satisfaction, I must say." She smiled and the worry disappeared. "Do you trust me? I have to talk to others. We must get ready. You need to rest. Tell me."

"Oh, yes, ma'am! I have to save my baby!" Rosetta exclaimed before Laura had a chance to speak. Laura wanted to throw herself into Mrs. Haskell's arms, hold her tightly and breathe in the fresh scent of her night-clothes. She was tired, felt so alone even though she had Rosetta at her side—how wonderful it would be to give herself over to another's care. "Yes," she said, echoing Rosetta's strong reply.

"Good," Mrs. Haskell said. "Both of you go to sleep now. I will wake you in the morning. And don't worry. The Lord will keep us all." She got up, moved the chair away, and picked up her candle. The light moved with her up the stairs, flickered, then disappeared as the trapdoor dropped. They were in pitch darkness again.

"Come on," Laura said to Rosetta. "Try to rest." And they lay back on the rough woolen blanket as if it had been the finest down and fell into dreamless sleep.

Chapter Sixteen

Hidden Away

"You be careful with that trunk. I've got some of my finest duds in there, don't want them shook up. Raise it up slowly onto the wagon, then we'll do the same with the other one. I want us on the road by noon."

Colonel Smithfield's voice was muffled but audible. Some other men made grunting sounds as they lifted the trunks onto the wagon. Laura could imagine him standing in Mrs. Haskell's kitchen door, dressed fine as a peacock, brandishing his cane as he gave directions for the moving of his possessions. Already, back at the meadow where the exhibition had been set up, the tents would be torn down, folded and stacked, the Hand of Destiny packed away. In a few hours all that would be left of the exhibition would be the memories people carried in their heads and the trodden-down grass where they had walked to see the sights.

The trunk dropped down on the wagon and Laura, hidden inside, almost groaned. Already her legs, folded beneath her, were cramped, and rivulets of sweat ran down her back. She remembered the caged animals at the exhibition and understood their sad eyes. A voice called out, and once more she was shaken as the wagon jerked to a start. But when she pressed her eye to the small opening Mr. Haskell had drilled into the side of the trunk for air, her view was blurred. All she could see was sunlight and shadows, nothing at all distinct. *Poor Rosetta,* she thought. She would be even more cramped in Colonel Smithfield's other trunk. Would the baby be all right?

But there had seemed to be no other way for them to get away. Earlier, in the hidden room when they awoke to the sound of tapping on the trapdoor above, Laura still half expected to see Mr. Higgins's triumphant face there, officers with badges standing beside him. But it was Mrs. Haskell again, fully dressed, her pale hair pulled into a bun on the back of her neck. Behind her, dawn glowed through the shutters of the parlor. She had food for them, cool milk, bread and side meat, and she said as she set it on the table, "Eat. You will have a long journey and you will need your strength." Then she told them the plan.

They would hide in Colonel Smithfield's trunks. "They are roomy," she told them, "padded inside." Mr. Haskell was already drilling holes in them so that they would be able to breathe. Most of Colonel Smithfield's clothes he would leave there and send for later. Men from the exhibition would load the trunks and then join the other departing wagons, passing right under Mr. Higgins's nose, wherever he might be watching the road.

"Why is he doing this?" Laura had asked. "Why does he care?"

Mrs. Haskell smiled. "As a favor to me, partly—we've known each other a long time. But more, I think, because he believes it's the right thing. 'Of course I'll help,' he said to me with a sparkle in his eye. 'I will take great delight in fooling some slave catcher. Despicable creature, preying on others. Why does he think he has the right? How could I, after all I've seen of the world, say this one is better than that one, this one should *own* the other? Yes, I will help these poor children, do everything in my power to see that they escape.'"

They waited at the edge of the light that came through the square above while Mrs. Haskell hurried about upstairs. They heard whisperings, the sounds of horses' hooves thumping on dry ground, the rattle of a wagon coming to a stop. Finally Mrs. Haskell's face appeared once again, and she said softly, "Come up.

We're ready." And they left their prison chamber and stepped back into the parlor one last time.

Miss Spurgeon stood by the door, her hair as red as fire, lit by the rising sun behind her. "It is time now," she said, pointing to the gaping trunks in the middle of the floor. "The men are here. Colonel Smithfield is waiting. You must get in."

She stood aside. Laura and Rosetta slowly approached the trunks. *Oh, Lord, I can't do it!* Laura suddenly thought. To step inside, kneel down, feel the lid close over her head, with only one small peephole to give her light and air—it seemed too awful, like being buried alive.

Miss Spurgeon must have seen her shoulders shaking. "It's all right, my dear," she said, rushing up to press her against her bosom. "You will be inside only a little while, until the wagon is back with the others at the exhibition. There is no other way. That terrible man will be watching. Come now, climb inside. We will pray for you. You must go."

Laura looked up, saw the tears gathering in the corners of Miss Spurgeon's eyes. Comforted, she pressed her lips to Miss Spurgeon's cheek and smelled the sweet scent of lavender she would remember all her life. Then, smiling to reassure Rosetta as well as herself, she climbed into the trunk and bent down, and Miss Spurgeon pulled the lid over her. The clasp locked into place. "Call in the carrier," Miss Spurgeon's muffled voice came through the small opening in the trunk. "We're ready."

They bounced along over the road toward the meadow where the other wagons and carts of the exhibition would be waiting, already hitched up to the horses. Laura shuddered to think that they might be passing right in front of Mr. Higgins's eyes that very moment, but no one called out for them to stop. The only voices she heard, murmuring too low for the words to be understood, were those of the men who had lifted up the trunks and placed them on the wagon, unaware of what was inside.

But when they reached the meadow and the wagon tilted down the hill, finally coming to rest on level ground, there came another voice that Laura recognized immediately. The voice of Tobias. It was he who called out firmly, "Careful now. You don't want to go upsetting the colonel's finery, would you? There'll be the devil to pay if you do." Laura's heart felt bigger than the trunk that contained her.

She was picked up again, then dropped with a thud. The horses neighed as they were led away. Laura tried to look through the opening, and though there was a breath of cooler air coming in, she saw only shadows. *What if no one comes to let us out?* she thought. Colonel Smithfield had stayed behind at Mrs. Haskell's to pack away his things. How much longer would she and Rosetta have to stay there cramped up in the trunks, nearly breathless, before he returned?

She heard Tobias's voice again, softer this time, barely more than a whisper. "Miss?" he called. "Are you all right? I'll undo the clasp now. Don't be afraid."

But suddenly she *was* afraid, wanted to bury herself deeper into the trunk's darkness to hide. Tobias knew they were there. Who else? She had trusted Mrs. Haskell and Colonel Smithfield, and she had no reason not to trust Tobias. Yet she still wondered in that moment before Tobias got the trunk's clasp open whether Mr. Higgins would be standing next to him ready to take Rosetta away, perhaps arrest Laura, too.

Those thoughts faded when she looked up and saw Tobias's smiling face, his hair bright even in the low light. "Well, look what I've found," he said, teasing, and reached out to take her arm. She straightened, stood, and held on to Tobias for a moment, slightly dizzy. Then she said, "Help Rosetta. She probably needs it more than I do. It's two of them cramped up inside."

"I'll be just fine," Rosetta said, standing once the lid was up. "And this baby been through a lot and don't know a thing about it, won't believe a word when I tell it later on." She lifted her skirts and stepped outside.

"We'll be going soon," Tobias said. He leaned against the center tent pole with folded arms as if it were nothing unusual for him to watch two girls spring from a pair of trunks as if by a magician's hand. "This is the colonel's office," he said. Laura followed his gaze to the tent and saw a folding table that served as a desk, two chairs, boxes, and another trunk. "His wagon is just outside. That's where you'll ride. It's already hitched and ready to go."

"We don't want to put him out," Laura said. "Isn't there some other place we can ride?"

"It's the colonel's *orders*," he said. "Nobody would dare question them. The colonel said, 'I'll lie out under the stars. It will be like in the old days when we didn't even have tents over our heads.' I think he's enjoying all this. I haven't seen him step so lively in a long while."

"What about the others? What will they think?"

Tobias pushed himself away from the tent pole and shrugged. "Probably won't. Nothing surprises you after you've been in this business for a while. The foreigners don't understand a word anyway, and the others, well, they've seen folks come and go before." He stopped and his face became serious. "It's the others we'll have to worry about, the visitors to the exhibition. They won't be expecting to see two ladies riding around with this bunch. You'll have to stay hidden most of the day. At night it'll be different. You can come out and no one will see."

Suddenly he turned. "It's time," he said. "Let me look." He went to the tent flap, pulled it back, and stuck his head out. Laura saw the side of a painted wagon, a faded banner with letters that spelled out SMITHFIELD'S but nothing more. Tobias motioned to them, and they hurried up behind him, eager to be away from the imprisoning trunks. "It looks clear," he said. "Follow me and don't dally." He walked through the opening, climbed up, and pulled back the flaps that covered the entrance to the wagon. Rosetta and Laura followed him inside. "Stay here," he said, whispering once again. "No one will bother you. I'll be back later." And with that, he was gone.

Laura and Rosetta stood in the middle of the wagon. Bright rugs spread beneath their feet. Silken banners hung from the metal frame that bore up the canvas top. There were two narrow cots, a chest, and another trunk. Clothes hung topsy-turvy from a line, and over all lay the heavy sweet scent of tobacco, like fruit too ripe.

"Lord have mercy," Rosetta said. "If my mama could see me now. She'd think for sure I'd been stolen away by the gypsies!" And for the first time in what seemed like ages, they fell into each other's arms, laughing uncontrollably, until they finally fell down on the beds and buried their heads in the pillows to stop the sound.

Chapter Seventeen

Good-bye

So they traveled with Colonel Smithfield's World-Famous Traveling Exhibition through back woods and country roads in a haze of late-summer heat. Dust trailed behind them like a bright banner, though sudden storms, crackling with lightning, would turn the road into a muddy trail. Asters, blue as the sky, bloomed along the way. Every day or so they would stop, unload the wagons, and set up the tents, and the Hand of Destiny would slowly turn again before eager sightseers in time to Colonel Smithfield's resonant voice.

During daylight, Laura and Rosetta remained in Colonel Smithfield's wagon, hidden from view. Laura mended clothes for the others as best she could in the dim light, and Rosetta sat content by her side, listening to Tobias's description of the countryside. On traveling days, he drove. "These girls will be your special responsibility," Colonel Smithfield had told him when they first started out, and Tobias had accepted the task eagerly, asking the girls over and over again, "Are you comfortable, did the last bump upset you?" and bringing them cool drinks of water whenever they passed a spring. Just the sound of his voice still thrilled Laura, and Rosetta, noticing, warned her, "Don't you go getting too sweet on that boy. We'll be gone soon. You'll never see him again and your heart will be broke."

At night it was different. With the crowds gone and the dust settling, they could come out of the wagon into the purpling light, stretching as if after a long nap. If a stream ran nearby, they washed their clothes at its edge, and sometimes, when no one else was around, they took off their shoes and stockings and stepped into the water, holding their dresses high. Back at the camp, fires would be lit, and the smell of frying food would drift out to them. Ravenous, they would hurry back to the wagon, hang out their clothes, then sit with the others for the evening meal they all shared.

They would go to bed early, climbing back into the curtained wagon, Tobias always nearby. Just before letting the canvas flap fall, Rosetta would say, "There it is, the North Star. Please, dear Jesus, let it be lighting my Samson's way."

They got to know the others. The acrobats with their strange-sounding names who always sat a little apart, peering off into the darkness as if looking for some familiar sight. The clown who tottered around the camp on his stumpy legs, teasing, joking, angering the others so that they would order him sharply away.

And of course there was Tobias, never very far from them. While he drove the wagon, his words were whipped back beneath the canvas by the wind, and he told them of all the places he had visited with the exhibition, the people he had met. He told them about himself as well, the jobs he had pursued—salesman door to door, portrait painter, repairer of pots and shoes—until he had met Colonel Smithfield, who had offered him the job of trick rider. Profile cutting was just something extra he did on the side. Listening to his words, Laura could practically see him leaping upon the prancing horse; and once during the day, despite the danger, she slipped out of the wagon and peered through a hole in the canvas to see him fly around the tent.

It couldn't last, of course, that magical time. Alone in the wagon with Rosetta, Laura would think again of Mr. Higgins and his pursuit, and she would look out beneath the canvas flap at the crowd, searching for his face. At night, after voices were quiet, she'd listen for frantic hoofbeats on the road until she'd finally fall asleep. So when Colonel Smithfield knocked on the frame of the wagon, pulled the canvas back, and said, "Well, ladies, how are you this lovely evening?" she guessed all too easily why he had come.

"Just fine," she said politely, stepping aside for him to climb up. Rosetta moved to the rear of the wagon, eyes somber as if she, too, suspected the reason for his visit.

He took a seat on one of the beds, pushed back his hat, and rested both hands on the head of his cane. He seemed as reluctant to continue as they to hear his words. Finally he said, "This is as far as we go. I have made arrangements for you. Others—you need not know their names—will be waiting for you to guide you across the river, and you will be met on the other side and helped to Philadelphia. It is still dangerous, but perhaps not so much as before. Many others have gone this way." He was silent for a moment, his knuckles white upon the cane. "I wish I could take you all the way myself, but that is impossible. You will have to trust in fate." He chuckled. "The Hand of Destiny will guide you. Everything will turn out for the best in the end."

He stood then, brushed off their thanks with a wave of his hand, and climbed down from the wagon. "Be ready at nightfall," he said. "Take only what you absolutely need. Tobias will drive you." And with that he walked away into the crowd.

It took them no time to pack a satchel. One dress for each, an extra pair of stockings, undergarments—they needed no more. Laura tucked the profile Tobias had cut of her carefully inside. Then they waited. The heat beneath the canvas was stifling, and though they heard once the distant roll of thunder, no relief came. They did not speak, seated on the narrow beds watching the light fade from the canvas walls as night descended. Finally it was time to go.

"You can come out now." It was Tobias's voice, soft by the flap of canvas. He pulled it back, and they could see him in the fading light. He smiled to reassure them. "The crowd is gone now," he said. "The way is clear. But we must hurry. There is still a long drive to where the others will be waiting."

Helping them down, he guided them over the weedy ground to a carriage, hitched to two of the horses that pranced in the show with Tobias on their backs. They were settling back into the darkness of the carriage when Colonel Smithfield's face appeared in the window. His usual smile was gone and there was sadness in his eyes. "Take care of yourselves, my dears. We will miss you. God help you on your way." He reached into his pocket and drew out a small leather bag in which coins rattled. "Here, take this," he said to Rosetta. "You may need it for your journey." She did not protest as he pressed the bag into her hand; she closed her fingers over it, and he turned away. Joining the others who stood on a grassy rise, he raised his hand in farewell. Tobias strapped the horses, and then they were away.

They rode through the dark night with only lightning bugs and a few stars to guide them. The moon had not yet risen, and heavy branches hung low over the roadway. "Lordy me," Rosetta said, "where are we going now? I don't think this baby of mine is ever going to get any true rest."

Laura tried to reassure her. "It won't be too much longer," she said. "Others will meet us, carry us across the river, then take you on to Philadelphia. I'll go back on the train."

Tears gathered in Rosetta's eyes, and she said, "I never spoke these words out loud before, but they've been a pain in my heart the whole time. What if he ain't there? Samson I mean. What if they caught him, sent him back? Then what will I do?"

Laura reached across the carriage and took both of Rosetta's hands in hers. "Don't even think such a thing," she said. "Of course he will be there, waiting with open arms. I know it. A few more days and you will be with him. Hush now and try to get some rest."

The carriage lurched, went down a bumpy bank, then stopped. Laura half expected to see Mr. Higgins's leering face appear in the window with a cry of triumph, but the eyes she saw in the darkness were Tobias's. "We're here," he whispered. "The others are waiting. Give me your satchel," and he reached out to help them down.

Figures lurked under the edge of the trees. There was a glint of water and the sulfur smell of a nearby bog. A boat would be anchored somewhere off in the darkness, ready to ferry them to the far side. Suddenly Laura did not want to go on. They had come so far, trusted so many others—how could they be sure their luck would continue? Would fate suddenly turn against them?

She stepped closer to Tobias, heard him catch his breath, and felt his arms suddenly around her. She knew then that it wasn't the fear of strangers that made her hesitate but the thought of leaving him. There were no words to tell him so, and he would not know of the ache in her heart. But he must have felt something, for he reached down and kissed her forehead and said, "Everything will be all right. You'll see. A year from now this will all seem like a dream. Maybe you'll come to see another show and I'll be there."

She nodded, though she knew it wasn't true, then turned and walked toward the waiting band of figures. The last she saw of Tobias was the back of his bright head as he drove the ready horses up the bank and off into the darkness.

Chapter Eighteen

Back Home

She leaned back against the wicker seat. The train whistle screeched in her ears, and the seat scratched her neck, but she hardly noticed, too exhausted to care. She had slept little the night before. Once Tobias had driven away, the figures had emerged from the darkness and guided them along a swampy path to the water's edge, then paddled them across the river. No one had spoken. The only sounds were the slap of water against the sides of the wooden boat and the croak of bullfrogs in the weeds. The moon rose just as they reached the other side.

"Girl, you come with us," a voice said to Rosetta as they stepped from the boat. "The others will take you to Baltimore, miss." A man stepped forward, tall, dressed all in black, with kindly eyes. His voice had the deep rumble of a preacher's voice during a Sunday morning sermon. "There are patrols near the bridge," he said. "We need to hurry."

"Oh!" Laura said, reaching out for Rosetta. All the tribulations they had been through were intended to get Rosetta to Philadelphia, safe from the hands of Mr. Higgins, but somehow she had never really thought of their parting. Now they must separate, and forever. Despite what comforting words they might try to say to each other, they knew that there would be no reunion. Wounds between people would not heal in so short a time. Men like Mr. Higgins would continue to prowl country roads and city streets looking for runaway slaves. Rosetta must get away, with no thought of return, and Laura must go back home. She enfolded Rosetta in her arms. Tears came. "Good-bye," she said through the blur. "Take care of the baby."

"Lord, I will. Can't let nothing hurt it now, we come so far, all three of us." Rosetta's eyes, too, were wet. "You go on back home now. I'll be just fine." And with one last squeeze of their hands, they parted. Darkness closed down and footsteps faded away.

The train whistle screamed again in her ear. Hot air blew in from the windows, scattering ashes from the engine over her skirt. Across the aisle, a man stared at her, and she drew her satchel closer, thinking of the coins that lay in the bottom. She had just enough money left to hire a carriage to take her from the train's end to Uncle Jesse and Aunt Charity's farm.

And wouldn't they be surprised! She could just imagine sitting down at the kitchen table with them, Aunt Charity white-faced with concern, Uncle Jesse quietly smoking while his foot tapped nervously on the floor, telling them of her and Rosetta's travels. So much had happened—it was hard even for her to believe.

In a few days her brother would return, as sullen as ever, so different from Tobias, to drive her home through woods still green, though the dry scent of autumn would already be in the air. When they arrived, her papa would give her a big hug, lifting her off the ground, but her mother would take one look at her and exclaim, "My Lord, look at you, brown as an Indian! Didn't you wear your bonnet to keep the sun off your face? Come in this house and take off your clothes. You're going to have a milk bath right this minute." She smiled to herself, relaxed, and, despite the noise and the heat and the cinders in her lap, fell asleep on the prickly seat.

Chapter Nineteen

The Letter

Aunt Charity and Uncle Jesse arrived the day before Christmas. "Well, now, aren't you a sight for sore eyes," Laura's papa said to them as they drove their wagon up to the front door. He helped Aunt Charity down and gave her a hug and then shook hands with Uncle Jesse. "Come on in," he said. "You must be tired after the journey. Harriet?" he called to Laura's mother. "Where are you? We've got kinfolks here that need warming and feeding."

Laura's mother rushed out the door, eyes aglow, arms open in welcome. "I was just trying to get my apron over my head before I came out," she said. "I must look a sight after standing in that hot kitchen day and night for a week." She brushed back her hair, gave Aunt Charity a peck on the cheek, and let herself be hugged briefly by Uncle Jesse.

"Well, look at thee!" Aunt Charity exclaimed as Laura came rushing down the steps behind her mother. She took her by the shoulders and held her out as if she were examining a piece of fine stitchery. "Two inches taller at least since we saw thee last summer. Thou are almost grown."

Laughing, Laura put her arms around Aunt Charity and kissed her cheek. But before she could say a word, her mother said, "Lord, if she'd only act it. Sometimes I think she's still a child. Stubborn, wandering over all this plantation without a care for caution, visiting the slaves' cabins—you've never seen the like. Worse, I'd say, after she came back from that visit with you, Charity. Whatever did you let her do? Brown as bark on a tree, she must have run wild in the fields. 'No young man is going to want an Indian,' I tell her, but she doesn't pay a bit of mind."

Aunt Charity did not respond but squeezed Laura's hand as they walked up the steps together and went inside.

They ate a simple supper. Afterward, the men sat smoking, talking of crops and rain, while Laura and her mother and Aunt Charity cleared the table. Henry was included in the men's conversation and sat proud as a peacock voicing his opinions. He still teased Laura, though not as much, and while she had been tempted to say to him, "You don't know a thing about the world beyond these fences, you don't know the sights I have seen," she never spoke to him of Rosetta and the secret roads they had traveled together. The memory of that journey was in a closed part of her heart, and she would keep it there always as a treasure.

"Whew, I'm about worn out," Aunt Charity said as she untied the towel she had put around her waist to keep from soiling her dress. "I've got to get to bed soon or I won't be a bit of help tomorrow. Laura?" she said, turning. "Are thou coming up, too?"

"I might as well," Laura said. "You know how Mama is—works herself to death every Christmas even though there are plenty of willing hands around. She wants to do it all herself." Aunt Charity laughed and said good night to her sister, who only sniffed and continued working at the stove. Laura said, "Good night, Mama. Don't work too late," then followed Aunt Charity up to bed.

The knock on her door came later. Laura had already brushed her hair and said her prayers and was just about to snuff out her candle when she heard the light rapping. "Yes?" she called out, but when she heard no answer, she got up from her bed and hurried across the floor in just her nightgown to open the door. Aunt Charity stood there with her hair falling around her shoulders, dressed in the old familiar wrapper she wore back home. "Come in," Laura said, "before you catch your death of cold. It's freezing out in the hallway."

Aunt Charity stepped inside. "I hope I didn't get thee up," she said. "I saw thy light beneath the door."

"Oh, no, ma'am. I was still up. I'm glad you came.

Come get under the covers." Laura led her to the bed, pulled back the quilts, and helped Aunt Charity climb onto the soft feather mattress. Then she got in herself and sank back among the pillows. "There, now," she said, "we can have our very own visit. I *have* missed you."

"And I, too," Aunt Charity said. "But thou can come again next summer. It isn't *that* far away."

Laura laughed. "I doubt if Mama would let me. She's still going on about how I look. Even now sometimes I catch her looking at me real close like she wonders what I might be thinking."

"Well, don't thee tell her," Aunt Charity said. "She did that to me when we were children, always wanted to know what was going on, whether it was any of her business or not. I did love to fool her and she'd get mad as a setting hen." Laura laughed and Aunt Charity shushed her, saying, "Be quiet or she'll hear us, and then I won't be able to give thee thy gift."

"What gift?" Laura said, wondering what special treat Aunt Charity might have hidden in her pocket.

"This," she said, and pulled out a crumpled piece of paper. She pressed it out on the counterpane but the wrinkles remained. The paper was stained, torn at the corner—an envelope, Laura saw now, though it bore no seal. "It has gone through who knows how many hands, but it finally got to us. I would say it's the next thing to being a miracle. Here, take it. It's for thee."

Laura carefully opened the envelope and pulled out the letter. "Oh, Aunt Charity!" she said when she glanced at the bottom and saw the name. Her eyes filled with tears so, at first, she could not see the words. Then she wiped them away and began to read.

Dear Laura,

Well, won't you be surprised to hear from me, at least if this letter gets through. Folks going back to help others say they'll take it but they can make no promises about where it will end up. I'll pray, though. The Lord got us through many a hard time on the road. For sure, He can direct a little letter.

Maybe it'll be more of a surprise to see me writing. Yes, reading, too. The preacher's wife, she's teaching me. Nicest lady in the world, reminds me of you, though she's got a funny way of saying things, like most people here. Canada, that's a funny name, isn't it? I never knew how far away it was, or how cold. Sometimes I think, "Lord, if I could just sweat a little I'd be happy," but then I think what it was like to be there working in the heat, and I know I don't really mean it.

It was a long journey getting here. After that night by the river when we saw each other last, some of my people, kind ones, hid me out for two days, then got me to Philadelphia, where there was a house I could stay in without fear, though they said, "Don't go outside, there are still slave catchers around, and some of our own people might betray you." I thought of that mean Mr. Higgins, and I didn't stick my nose once out the door.

Then Samson came. Lord, was I glad to see him! All bright and healthy, the scars on his back healed. He had a hard time getting through, but he made it. We took the train to Canada to a place where others who had escaped welcomed us and helped us settle in. We feel safe at last.

The baby came in November. I never expected so much pain, but when I looked at her, hair all curly and dark as sweet molasses, little hands grabbing for me, I forgot all that. Now I have two things to love, Samson and little Laura.

Yes, that's her name. Laura. I didn't think you'd mind. I wanted to name her after you. She's a pretty thing. Maybe one day you'll see her. Who knows what will happen in this life? Just think what we went through.

I'd better stop now. My hand is getting tired. The words don't come easy. Maybe you'll write me one of these days and your letter will get through. I'll pray.

Till then, your true and loving friend,
Rosetta

For a long time Laura sat in bed rereading Rosetta's letter. Quietly, giving her a squeeze, Aunt Charity got up and slipped out of the room. The candle sputtered down, and the fire in the grate dimmed, but Laura felt no chill. Finally she got up, walked across the floor to the chest that stood by the window, and took down the basket that rested on the top. Her childhood treasures lay inside. Polished pebbles from a creek bed, the wasps' nest her brother had brought her, animal teeth bleached white by the sun. Reaching below them, she carefully took out the sheet of folded paper, opened it, and saw herself there—her profile cut so lifelike by Tobias's shears, until now her most precious keepsake.

She took one last look at Rosetta's letter, then put it in the envelope and enclosed it with her likeness, one more treasure to last a lifetime. She put the folder back on the bottom of the basket, laid the nest and the pebbles on top, and set it back on the chest. Scurrying across the ice-cold floor, she snuffed out the candle, climbed quickly into bed, and fell immediately to sleep. Her dreams were of babies nestled in their mothers' arms and protected by angels' wings, and she woke to the new day rested and with joy.